Also by Ron Schwab

MOUTH OF HELL
The Law Wranglers

a novel by
RON SCHWAB

Poor Coyote Press
An imprint of Leafcutter Publishing Group

MOUTH OF HELL
by Ron Schwab

Poor Coyote Press
PO Box 6105
Omaha, NE 68106
www.PoorCoyotePress.com

Cover Art: "Breaking Through the Lines" by Charles Schreyvogel

ISBN: 1-943421-18-8
ISBN-13: 978-1-943421-18-3

MOUTH OF HELL

The Law Wranglers

1

JOSH RIVERS SENSED he was being followed. He hadn't caught as much as a glimpse of his stalkers, but there were two or three, he was fairly certain. His buckskin gelding seemed skittish, but the pack mule that trailed behind was unperturbed. He scolded himself for not having recruited his brother, Cal, for the mission. Cal, a former scout for Brevet General Ranald Mackenzie, would have pinpointed the pursuers an hour ago and likely taken them down. But his little brother had been smitten by a young woman they ransomed from the Comanche and, as far as Josh knew, was still holed up on her ranch in northeast New Mexico.

His rough-cut sibling had even clumsily midwifed the birth of Erin McKenna's half-blood baby on the trail. Choosing the name for baby girl Willow had welded the final link in the chain that locked Cal to Erin—for now, anyway. Josh was skeptical of his brother's attempt to sink roots.

He tossed another look over his shoulder. There was a possibility the trackers were not hostile. He had nudged the buckskin south from the Red River on the Texas side of the border with New Mexico several hours back. Perhaps they were

Kwahadi Comanche confirming he was not accompanied by unwelcome visitors. The cavalry had launched another campaign to drive wayward Kiowa and Comanche back to the reservation near Fort Sill, Oklahoma and, of course, to conquer war chief Quanah and his band, who still ravaged Texas and eastern New Mexico and remained defiant. This would not be a time for trusting. Josh's destination was Little Buffalo Canyon, which a Mexican messenger had informed him was about three hours due south of a clump of large cottonwoods near a sharp turn in the river's course. It would be the only canyon in his path, he was told, and Quanah's emissaries were to rendezvous with him there. He should be less than an hour away. He reined in the buckskin as he approached a narrow ravine that was carved through a wall of cliffs that rose from the parched prairie like a rocky fortress and blocked his southward journey. It offered a natural passageway. It also presented a potential trap for the unwary. He decided he had no choice, and he nudged his horse ahead, entering the cut slowly with his eyes on the cliffs that reached some twenty-five or thirty feet above. But the attack came from behind him, and he heard the rifle fire in the same instant he felt the bullet slice the flesh between his neck and left shoulder. Josh pulled his Winchester from the saddle scabbard and swung his horse around, wincing from the pain as he lifted the rifle to his shoulder, suddenly aware of the blood soaking his shirt. He fired off two quick shots at the rider, who was some fifty yards behind him. The shooter wheeled his horse and raced away from Josh's fire. Josh, in turn, headed his horse for the exit from the gap.

He reined the horse carefully over the rough and rock-strewn arroyo floor, casting his eyes for a likely spot to seek cover and staunch his bleeding, for he could feel the weakness crawling through his limbs and fuzziness seeping into his head. Another shot rang out, echoing through the bluffs above, and he caught sight of another gunman on a ragged ledge some fifteen feet up in the rocks and thirty yards in front of him. A second shot scattered shale and kicked up dust a few feet from the buckskin's front hooves, and Josh slipped off of the horse and slapped the gelding's flank to move the animal out of the line of fire. The horse lunged forward and galloped down the trail with the mule following close behind. He staggered toward a fissure in the rock wall. It was barely wide enough to admit his rangy frame, but he squeezed in, protected now on three sides—also unable to get a bead on his attackers. While he waited, he pulled his hunting knife from its sheath and sliced off pieces of his shirt and pressed one fragment onto the double-holed wound created by the entrance and exit of the bullet. At least, he thought, the wound should have bled clean. This seemed to staunch the bleeding some. He could hear rock rattling and crunching on the arroyo floor, but his hideaway in the crevice offered only a narrow view straight in front of him. His cramped quarters made it difficult to maneuver the carbine into firing position. His wounded shoulder was on fire and stiffening, so he set it aside and pulled his Colt from its holster and held it in readiness. He could hear the low rumble of voices not far from the opening. He figured he had a fair chance of holding them off a spell, because he didn't see how they could get a clear shot at him without stepping into his line of fire. On the other hand, blood still trickled from his wound, and his water supply had departed with Buck and the pack mule. They could wait him out if they were not in a hurry. Well, he didn't have a choice. He would find out soon if they were into the waiting game.

He stood there silently for nearly an hour, keenly aware the blood flow from his wound was increasing. His head was swimming from vertigo, his legs weakening, and he knew he couldn't hold out much longer.

Suddenly, a high-pitched whiny voice broke the silence. "Hey there, Rivers. We've waited long enough. Time for you to come out and talk a spell."

He did not respond.

"You hear me, Rivers? We ain't got time to play hide and seek no more. There's three of us and one of you. We'll blast you out of there if we have to. We just want to have a word with you, and then we'll be on our way."

"If you wanted to have a friendly chat, why did you ambush me?" he yelled back.

"Just wanted to get your attention, that's all."

"One of you can walk out in front of my line of fire, and I'll have my end of the discussion from here."

"You think we're damn fools? We ain't getting in nobody's line of fire. Forget that shit."

"Then I guess you'll have to come in firing, because I'm not going anywhere." They'd just as well have it out, he decided. He wasn't going to be on his feet much longer. He was comfortable and accurate with his Colt revolver, thanks to his father's insistence that all five of his brood, including Josh's sister, Tabby, meet the patriarch's rigid standards for handling firearms. He was confident he would take one or two of his adversaries with him.

His body was failing him, and he opted for surprise, suddenly lunging from his hideaway with his revolver ready to fire. There were three of them clustered off to the left side, not more than twenty-five feet away. Startled, they clawed frantically for their guns. Josh fired two quick shots and dived to the ground, rolled and raised his pistol for another shot. But his attackers were not in sight. His head was spinning, but he looked again and realized that all three men were sprawled on the ground. *What the hell?* Had he nailed three men with two shots? Then he saw the arrow shafts protruding from their bodies like pins from a cushion, and he could make out shadowy figures creeping slowly toward the fallen men. Darkness devoured him, and his pistol slipped from his hand and clattered on the rocky ground where he collapsed.

2

DANNA SINCLAIR LEANED back in her new oak swivel-chair and gazed out the open window that gave her a generous view of Santa Fe's Plaza and delivered the tantalizing smell of fresh-baked breads and other tempting morsels offered by the vendors along the streets and walkways. It was early May, but it was unseasonably warm, and although the thick adobe walls would keep the room comfortably cool throughout the remainder of the spring, she was feeling a little heat at the back of her neck.

Danna plucked an emerald-green ribbon from her desk drawer and gathered her long strawberry-blonde hair into what some westerners were starting to characterize as a ponytail. It left her with not so much of a professional appearance, she mused, but it was a hell of a lot more comfortable. Danna was well into the second year of her partnership with Josh Rivers, and she had prospered since abandoning her office in tiny Madison, which was located in the isolated northeast corner of New Mexico Territory.

The chair, with a leather cover tacked over a soft, cotton seat pad, was her sole frivolity—a concession to the excessive time she spent sitting on her butt these days. The office was otherwise austerely furnished with a single set of barrister bookcases stacked from floor to ceiling on one plastered wall and two captain's chairs on the opposite side of her desk. Her law diploma from the University of Virginia and her bar admission certificate from the Territorial Court hung on the wall behind her, one on each side of a large Regulator clock.

Some days she envied her law partner, Josh Rivers, who had an uncanny ability to evade sit-down office time. She had met Josh when he associated with her on a case she was handling for the aunt of a young woman, Erin McKenna, who had been abducted by the Comanche. Her father had been killed during a Comanche raid and had died without leaving a will. Her father's brother, Oliver McKenna, had commenced legal action to have Erin declared dead and himself ruled as the only heir to her father's vast land holdings. Josh and his brother, Cal, had ransomed Erin from Comanche war chief, Quanah, and returned with the young woman and her infant daughter to Santa Fe just in time to demolish the uncle's claim. In the course of the case Danna and Josh had formed a business alliance, and the McKenna fee had given the new firm a good start.

An unexpected windfall from the McKenna ransom had been acquisition of a new firm client, Quanah, known by some as Quanah Parker, whose mother, Cynthia Ann Parker, had been abducted as a child and raised as a Comanche. Quanah had handed over a handsome retainer in gold nuggets to employ Josh to pave the trail to favorable peace terms for the Kwahadi band and its Comanche and Kiowa allies.

She glanced up at the wall clock, its pendulum ticking with unnecessary volume, she thought. Usually, she did not notice the timekeeper's rhythmic click-clack, but this morning she found it a bit annoying, as she waited for her next scheduled appointment to show up.

An unidentified agent of a prospective client had made the appointment, promising Linda de la Cruz, the firm's young secretary, Danna would want to talk with this person. There was an important and serious message to be delivered.

This had all piqued Danna's curiosity, but the client was due within five minutes if he was inclined to punctuality. If not, there would be a five-minute reprieve. After that, Danna would not accommodate the caller's visit. Danna Sinclair was nothing if not punctual.

3

THERE WAS A soft tapping on the office door. "Yes?"

Linda opened the door. "Your appointment, Mr. Clayborne Pierce, is here."

"Show him in."

Pierce entered the room, his dark, heavy-lidded eyes casting about the room, obviously checking out his surroundings— probably from force of habit—before he extended his hand to Danna. "Miss Sinclair?"

"I am pleased to meet you, Mr. Pierce."

She gestured to one of the chairs in front of her desk near the open window and sat down in her own chair across from him. Danna noted that the man was well-tailored, but his gray suit draped loosely on a bony frame. His face was sun-weathered and leathery, and a bushy, black mustache nearly hid his upper lip. When he had entered the room she observed he stood ramrod straight, suggesting a military history. In his boots he stood about six feet tall, so they were close to a match for height.

Danna got right to the point. "You're something of a mystery, Mr. Pierce. Whoever made your appointment declined to divulge your name. This all seems very clandestine."

"Let's just say I'm very careful. It's a matter of habit and occupation, you might say." He pushed back an unruly shock of black hair from his forehead.

Danna decided he was younger than she originally guessed. He was probably in his late thirties or early forties, aged prematurely by a hard, outdoor life, perhaps. She actually found him handsome in a very rugged, rough-hewn way. "And may I ask what occupation you are engaged in? I have a hunch your work is directly related to your visit here."

He gazed out the window a moment, like he was looking for something in the azure sky, before he turned back and spoke. "Some folks call me a bounty hunter. I prefer to identify myself as a private searcher. You see, while I might occasionally track down someone of the criminal ilk, I most often search for folk who have disappeared. More recently, I have found the hunt for Comanche captives to be quite profitable."

Danna was uncertain where this was leading. "My guess is that you have some military experience."

"West Point. Fourth Calvary. Served as a captain out of Fort Riley, Kansas until I decided I wasn't cut out for career army. After that I hired out to traders traveling on the Santa Fe Trail for protection services."

"And that led you to ransoming captives?"

"Yes, that and the good luck I ran into by teaming up with a young Tonkawa warrior on one of the freighter jobs."

"Tonkawa. The cannibals."

"So they say. But Screeching Owl has never tried to eat me, and as near as I can tell, he's most partial to buffalo ribs. He was a Comanche captive himself for almost three years before he escaped. He might have stuck around, but because the tribes are ancient enemies, he was never given status much above a slave. His band would adopt about anybody else into the tribe . . . whites, Negroes, Mexicans. Anybody but a Tonkawa."

Danna was growing impatient. She could not tell where this conversation was headed. "I am afraid I have other business waiting, Mr. Pierce. I have to ask why you require my legal services."

"I understand, ma'am, but it is quite the opposite. I think you . . . or I should say, your partner . . . may need my services."

Danna remained silent and looked at Pierce with annoyance.

"You see," Pierce said, "Screeching Owl knows the location of Josh Rivers's captive son."

Danna was taken aback and found she was untypically speechless for a moment. "He is alive then?"

"He was certainly alive two weeks ago."

"And how do you know this? Have you seen him?"

"Screeching Owl has a Comanche friend in the camp of the band that holds the boy."

"You said the Comanche hate the Tonkawa, and you are telling me your associate has a Comanche friend?"

"The type of friend who can be bought."

"So why have you chosen to speak with me about this? My partner is the one you should have contacted."

"First, I have learned that Mr. Rivers is currently absent from Santa Fe. He is also said to be quite obsessed about his missing son . . . understandably so. And some say he is not so civilized that he has totally abandoned the law of the gun. I was not comfortable with the possible irrationality of his reaction to this information . . . and, in particular, to my proposal."

"And how could you be certain of my reaction?"

"You sincerely empathize with your partner, I am sure, but you don't have the same emotional investment in his misfortune. I think I surmised correctly . . . you seem quite rational about this."

"You have a proposal you wish to have me carry to my partner?"

"Yes, I propose to ransom the Rivers boy. I will require one thousand dollars in advance for my services. An additional one thousand will be payable when I return with terms acceptable to Mr. Rivers, and I would expect the further sum of one thousand dollars upon return of the boy to his rightful family. If I cannot negotiate terms, I forfeit the final two payments, but if I am not successful in negotiating terms, I will inform your partner of the boy's location, and he may do as he will. Funds for the remaining payments would be held in an escrow account by a Santa Fe bank with appropriate instructions to disburse payment upon submitting evidence of satisfaction of the conditions. The fees are for my services. The ransom would be Mr. Rivers' additional cost."

"I'm doubtful Josh has that kind of money readily available."

"His father is a well-to-do rancher, and he has a brother who is a Denver banker. I have made it my business to learn about this family, and I suspect the child's life and future are priceless."

"Alright, I'll speak to Josh. Where can you be found?"

"I'll find you folks. You'll hear from me within a few days after Mr. Rivers returns to Santa Fe. I will know, and I will allow sufficient time for you to speak with him."

4

AFTER CLAYBORNE PIERCE departed, Danna left the office and strolled to the Exchange Hotel where she had promised to meet Tabitha Rivers for lunch. She waited for Tabby at a small table in the hotel's dining room. A special assignments reporter for *The Santa Fe New Mexican*, Tabby, the youngest and only female of the five Rivers siblings, shared a small home with Danna, although she stayed there so infrequently the lawyer and their black cat, Midnight, saw her only occasionally.

She did not know when Josh would return. He had said he was headed for West Texas, where he had arranged a rendezvous with Quanah's representatives. Several months ago Josh had met secretly with the Indian agent at Fort Sill, Oklahoma about terms under which Quanah would be willing to sign a peace treaty. These would include land and cattle for the Comanche and a promise of non-incarceration for the leaders. The agent thought such a plan might be achievable since Quanah and his followers were virtually the last Comanche holdouts and an embarrassment to the U.S. Army and the Grant administration. He had promised to pass word through the bureaucracy. That word would creep slowly, she knew, but Josh thought a breakthrough was near.

Danna had decided she would tell Tabby about her conversation with Pierce. She did not see an issue of confidentiality. Pierce was not a client, and she was a mere messenger. Tabby seemed to know everybody who ever passed through Santa Fe, and she might have heard of Pierce.

"You're someplace else."

Danna started. It was Tabitha, who was already slipping into the chair on the opposite side of the table, bearing her seemingly ever-present mischievous smile. Chestnut-colored hair, olive-skinned and petite, perhaps an inch or two short of five and a half feet, she turned the head of every male in Santa Fe. Danna didn't know anything about Tabby's mother, who had been murdered along with Josh's wife in the Comanche raid that had resulted in the abduction of the infant Michael, but from the looks of her daughter, the woman must have been of Spanish or Mexican descent.

"Sorry, I guess I was preoccupied."

"Is Josh back yet?" Before Danna could reply, the young Mexican waiter appeared, and they both ordered coffee and a plate of enchiladas.

"To answer your question," Danna said, "no, I'm not expecting him for at least three or four days."

"Another of his mystery trips . . . something you don't want to share with an up and coming journalist?"

"It's not a matter of 'want.' I can't . . . the attorney-client issue. A very important client."

"Somehow, I suspect there's a story there. You'll give me the scoop?"

"I can't promise, but I'll see what I can do."

"Well, I was hoping to see Josh before I leave, but it sounds like I may miss him. I'll be leaving for an extended time in a matter of a few days."

"You wasted your money on your half share of our home. You're never there."

"But I need a place to bunk when I'm in town . . . and somewhere to leave my things. And I think it's a good investment. Santa Fe will do nothing but grow in the years ahead."

"I'm not complaining. Midnight and I love the place, and I couldn't have purchased it on my own. So you're heading out on a new adventure? Secret destination?"

"Somewhat unknown. I'll be leaving with a cavalry detachment from Fort Union to join up with Colonel Ranald Mackenzie's forces out on the Staked Plains. Mackenzie's calling this the final campaign to either destroy or bring in Quanah and the remaining bands of Comanche and Kiowa that are still terrorizing western Texas."

The waiter returned with their meals, and by this time Danna was ravenous and turned her attention to her plate of enchiladas. The two women ate in silence for some moments before she spoke. "You're the only woman traveling with all those men. How'd you wangle that?"

"I took the idea to my editor and convinced him that I could use my gender to sell newspapers. He knows I can write better than any man on his staff. And a woman reporting from the battlefields is a novel idea, don't you think?"

"Yes, but it is a dangerous idea, also. You'll not only have to watch out for Comanche but your own traveling companions, as well. You'll have some who resent a woman's presence . . . and others who might seek to exploit the opportunities they envision with a beautiful woman in camp."

"I can handle it. I can ride better than most soldiers . . . and shoot better, too. Plus, I guarantee you I won't be wearing a frilly dress out there on the plains. Buckskins are more my style anyway."

Danna could see Tabby's dark eyes sparkle with enthusiasm as she spoke. The woman seemed not acquainted with fear. As to marksmanship, Danna's competitive spirit pushed her to challenge Tabitha to a match. Perhaps, when she returned from her assignment, Danna would do just that.

"I've even conjured up a name for the campaign," Tabby said. "In my first dispatch, I'm going to call it the 'Red River War.' Just wait, you'll see that term in the headlines."

"You're planning to make your career with this, aren't you?"

"Damn right. I'm the prototype for 'conniving bitch,' don't you think?"

They both laughed. Then Danna turned serious. "There's something you should be aware of."

"What?"

Danna told her about Clayborne Pierce and the proposed ransom and recovery of Michael Rivers. "Have you ever heard of this man?" Danna asked.

"I've not only heard of him, I've interviewed him."

"You're serious?"

"I guess it was about six months ago. He had ransomed ten-year-old twin boys who had been abducted during a raid on Don Miguel Estrada's estate. Pierce evidently has very good contacts within the Comanche bands. He had located these boys as their band was preparing to go to the reservation, so they were more dispensable to the Comanche at that point. They probably figured the boys would be found on the reservation anyway and decided to cash in, although it would not have been an easy decision, because after five years the boys would have been family by that time. Anyway, since the Estradas were prominent New Mexicans, my editor asked me to do a feature on the rescue . . . which incidentally turned out to be a second abduction."

"What do you mean?"

"The twins did not want to be rescued. They were now Comanche and wanted no part of a new family they barely remembered. The boys had to be bound and carefully guarded on the journey back to their parents' hacienda. After they were delivered to their natural parents they fought fiercely against the embrace of their parents and tried to escape. They finally had to be kept under lock and key . . . caged so to speak . . . until they could be tamed. I would like to write a follow-up story sometime, if the Estradas would permit it, to report on the twins' adjustment."

"It must have been a huge disappointment to the parents."

"Of course. And I couldn't help but think about little Michael. It's been four years. He would be nearly five years old now. He's Comanche, not Rivers. It's not going to be a happy reunion if Josh ransoms him."

"I'd never thought about that. What about Pierce? What did you think of him?"

"A little full of himself. Perhaps it's just confidence. He's a businessman, pure and simple. His work is not some altruistic crusade he's on. It's his path to a fortune. He's also smart enough, I'm sure, to see that his career is about burnt out. Within five years, the Comanche will all be on reservations. There will be no more need for his services. As to his character? He seemed to take pride in his work. I think his word is good. He comes off cold as stone. But I wouldn't expect him to be running a fraud. He must be pretty damn certain he's located Michael."

"What's Josh going to do when Pierce makes his proposal?"

"I hope he doesn't kill the man."

5

JOSH AWOKE TO the sight of two glowering Comanche faces, watching him like wolves with a cornered fawn. The soft glow of the sun was slipping over the canyon's rim, and it would be dark soon. A small fire crackled between him and the warriors, and the warriors squatted in front of it as they roasted some kind of meat on sticks. He noticed that both men wore only breechclouts with deerskin shirts. One had two blood-crusted scalps tucked in the rawhide strip that supported his breechclout, and the other displayed a hunk of flesh that showed more skin than hair. Josh decided that scalp must have belonged to a nearly bald man.

Then he caught sight of someone else walking quietly toward him from off to his left. The figure was slender and clad in buckskins and knelt by his side. He lifted himself up on his elbows and scooted back, resting against what he suddenly realized was Buck's saddle. Nothing was making any sense.

"How are you feeling?" It was a woman's voice. A familiar one.

"Confused."

"Are you hurting?"

He remembered his shoulder wound. "Not much, actually." He turned his head toward the voice and recognized her. "She Who Speaks?"

"Yes, of course. Quanah sent me to meet with you at Little Buffalo Canyon. That's where we're at. There is water and grass here . . . even a few trees. Plenty of deer and rabbit."

"How did I get here?"

"Scratching Turkey and Growling Bear brought you to the canyon. I waited here and set up camp and sent them up the trail to watch for you and to verify you were not being followed."

"Don't trust me?"

"There are others we do not trust who might suspect you are communicating with Quanah. Did you recognize any of the men?"

"I had only seconds to get a look. The one I shot . . . or thought I shot . . . looked familiar. I thought he might have been a man who worked for Oliver McKenna. I saw him near the courthouse when we were handling Erin McKenna's case."

"Be assured you did not shoot anyone. Neither of my companions would have taken the scalp of a man he had not killed. They carry three scalps."

He shifted his weight and winced when he felt the stab of pain in his neck and shoulder. It was nothing, though, compared to the agony he had endured before he blacked out. He ran his fingers over the tender flesh around his wounds. He found surprisingly little swelling beneath a layer of some kind of crusty substance that caked the skin.

"I treated it with a poultice I made from 'white man's foot' and other healing plants. The bleeding has been staunched. I will wrap it before you get up, but it is best to keep the wound uncovered as much as possible. The paste will do its job more effectively."

"Don't tell me you're some kind of medicine woman, too?"

"I have acquired some knowledge in the ministering of medicines during my time with the Comanche, but many of my band have greater faith in the ceremonies and chants of the traditional shamans. I am available to help, but I know my place in the order of things and assist only when someone comes to me and asks."

Suddenly he was aware of the dryness in his mouth and of an overwhelming thirst. As though reading his mind, She Who Speaks produced his canteen. "You need to drink," she said. "And then you will eat and sleep some more."

He raised himself up some. "The canteen was with my horse."

"Growling Bear recovered your horse and pack mule. They are staked in the grass near the stream."

"That was kind of him."

"Actually, he had hoped to claim the beasts, if you did not survive."

"Then I probably disappointed him."

"Probably. The buckskin is a fine animal."

He lifted the canteen to his lips and drank greedily until she plucked it from his hands. "Slowly," she admonished, placing the canteen at his side. "I will roast some venison over the fire and return shortly."

Later, the woman gave him a potion to drink. Whatever it was quickly made him drowsy. She assured him she would remain nearby in case he needed assistance. Nights were still cool on the Staked Plains, and she tucked one end of a buffalo robe under his body and then draped the remainder of it over his blanket, and he could not remember when he had last felt so comfortable and cozy. It was not difficult to handle this type of coddling.

She Who Speaks left for a spell and returned with her own buffalo robe and rolled it out next to him. "In the morning I will dress your wounds. Then you will get up and tend to your animals and prepare your own breakfast. After that, we will talk. My friends and I depart after one more night."

She Who Speaks rolled up in her robe and apparently dropped off to sleep instantly. Josh could feel the drug subduing him, and as he waited for it to take him into slumber, he thought of the woman who slept a few feet from his side. They had first met when he had journeyed into the Staked Plains to find and ransom Erin McKenna. He had been captured by Quanah and a Kwahadi war party and taken to their encampment in Palo Duro Canyon, and She Who Speaks had been sent to his tipi to discuss his fate.

She had been taken captive at age fourteen and adopted by the tribe. When Josh encountered her some six years later, She Who Speaks would have passed for full-blood Comanche. Other than being taller than most Comanche women, she had many Comanche features. She wore her sable hair long and braided. Her nose and facial features were softly aquiline and her flawless skin was no lighter than that of the many half-bloods found in Comanche camps. Slender and willowy, the woman was several steps above attractive, he thought.

At their first meeting, Josh had learned nothing about She Who Speaks's life before it began with the Comanche. He knew only that she had a small son and a husband, the latter of whom was killed during a cavalry attack that occurred while Josh was held prisoner. Unlike most Comanche women, She Who Speaks had carved out a position of some influence in Kwahadi hierarchy, apparently because of her skill as an interpreter and translator. She had informed Josh that his name and quest were known to the village elders and that Quanah had a mission for him also. She had sat in council with Josh and the Kwahadi leaders and acted as interpreter as they discussed the possible ransom of Erin McKenna. Quanah, during that time, denied knowledge about the young woman's whereabouts. Later, she had met with Josh and Quanah when the war chief proposed to retain Josh to negotiate acceptable terms of peace with the "white eyes."

Gold nuggets talked, and Josh had taken on the task subject to the condition that Erin McKenna be found and delivered to him for an agreed ransom. He had met She Who Speaks briefly again at the exchange several weeks later. It was then he had learned of the death of her husband. Lengths of her hair had been sliced away as a part of her mourning ritual. Understandably, their conversation had been brief and perfunctory.

Yes, this is an interesting woman, he thought, as he drifted off.

6

WHEN JOSH AWAKENED, the sun had not quite crawled over the canyon walls. He turned to see if She Who Speaks was still asleep. Her robe had disappeared, and there was no sign she had spent the night beside him. Her companions were still squatting by the fire, but he assumed they had abandoned their positions sometime during the night to catch some sleep, perhaps in shifts.

Josh rolled over and carefully raised himself up first on his knees, testing his strength. He found the pain in his shoulder surprisingly tolerable, just a residue of soreness and stiffness, so he awkwardly clambered to his feet. A wave of dizziness struck him but passed quickly. He noticed that the warriors were watching him with some interest, but their faces remained impassive. He caught sight of his gear and supplies stacked against a small cottonwood tree some ten paces away, near the bank of a narrow stream that split the canyon floor and snaked its way over a rocky bed that angled from north to south. He ambled over to the stream and knelt down and splashed water on his face. This woke him with a start. It was cold as ice, so it must be spring-fed from some source in the canyon, he figured.

Looking downstream he could see that the stream widened noticeably as it twisted southward. Then he spotted someone sitting on a ragged stone outcropping above the water, perhaps thirty yards away. As he focused, he realized it was She Who Speaks, her naked back turned his way. She had evidently been bathing in the frigid water and was now drying in the morning breeze that was plenty cool, too, he thought. He shook his head in disbelief and turned away and began fishing out his supplies.

He returned to the fire with a black, cast-iron skillet, a slab of bacon and a canvas bag of hardtack biscuits. He cut the bacon into thick strips, dropping the slices in the skillet, as the Indians watched curiously. Growling Bear's eyes widened, as the bacon started sizzling and crackling and the tantalizing scent drifted his way. Josh pulled the skillet back from the hot coals and stabbed one of the strips with his knife and held it out to the Comanche, signing with his free hand "to eat." Hesitantly, the Comanche took the bacon and studied it a few moments before taking a test bite. Meanwhile, Josh offered a slice to Scratching Turkey who, after watching Growling Bear's reaction, stuffed it into his mouth. Both of the warriors grunted with satisfaction and smiled agreeably. Josh offered hardtack to both, which they accepted with less suspicion. Soon they were all sharing bacon and biscuits like old comrades, and Josh trimmed more slices from the slab while his new friends waited.

"Smells good." The soft voice came from behind him.

Josh turned and looked up at She Who Speaks, who looked radiant in her buckskins this morning. "I have plenty," he said. "Sit down and join us."

"I shall." She sat down and helped her companions decimate the slab.

Josh decided that bacon was off the menu for the trip home. He got up and took care of the little cleaning up he had to do, while She Who Speaks spoke to the warriors in their Comanche dialect. In a few moments the two Comanche disappeared.

Shortly, she joined Josh. "I will tend to your shoulder, and then we can talk." She instructed him to sit down and lean back against the cottonwood. Then she cleaned the wounds, nodded with approval, and applied more of her poultice. "The wounds are doing very well . . . no sign of infection whatever."

"Thanks to the skill of my physician. You sound strangely professional for someone who claims to be Comanche."

She found her own spot next to the tree and rested her back against it, so she and Josh formed a rough right angle, neither facing the other. "My father was a physician. I suppose I have never forgotten his manner of speaking. Unlike most adopted members of the band, I have never forgotten or abandoned my language roots. I have a strange affinity for languages. Although Comanche, of course, have no written language, I learned it very quickly, and when white men came to the camp to trade . . . including the Comanchero thieves . . . I was quickly put to work translating. Many of these men were Mexican, and I began to pick up Spanish words. Then we had a Mexican captive in camp for nearly a year, and I was permitted to speak with him. He was eager to talk to me and help with the language because he had no one else to communicate with, and I was able to be his interpreter. Now I am reasonably fluent in five languages."

"Five? English, Comanche, Spanish and—?"

"German and Yiddish."

"Yiddish? That's beyond bizarre if you don't mind my saying so. I'm not even certain what that is."

"It is a variation of Hebrew with a German influence and a few other languages mixed in. I read Hebrew . . . I suppose I still could . . . but I am not fluent speaking the language. It was rarely spoken where I grew up. Yiddish was the language of our community."

"And where was that?"

"Germany. We were Jews."

"You're Jewish?"

"By birth, yes. By religion, I think not. I've adopted the gods of my tribe. They are convenient and make a certain sense."

"How did you end up here?"

"Following my father's dream. Tevel Chernik was a physician who decided he wanted to take his skills to America. My mother, Naomi, was a German school teacher, and she had a large family there. My father was stricken by the wanderlust at an early age and had immigrated to Germany from Poland, where he met and married my mother. He enjoyed a very successful medical practice in a small town on the Rhine. But America kept calling, and he was determined to answer. Mother resisted. I can still remember my parents' loud quarrels about immigrating, but my father was very strong-willed, and, in the end, he got his way. This was fine with me. It all sounded very exciting. I guess it turned out that way."

"I detect a bit of sarcasm."

"It wasn't enough for my father to settle with other Jews in New York. He insisted that we go west, and Santa Fe intrigued him. He was undaunted by the idea of a German Jew invading an entirely different culture. He declared that the language of medicine was universal and that he could do much good among the Mexicans and Indians there. So we travelled to St. Louis, eventually joined a small wagon train. While he was sometimes stern with my mother and me, Tevel . . . I have not spoken his name in more than eight years . . . it seems strange . . . Tevel made friends easily, and he put his skills to work during the journey, even delivering two babies. He was awed by the fact that no one seemed to mind his Jewishness."

"But you didn't make it to Santa Fe."

"No. A wheel broke on our wagon and we were separated from the main train. Several men stayed behind to help replace the wheel, but the Comanche burst from nowhere. And everyone died but me. My mother was raped many times and was scalped while still alive. My father and the others died before the scalping. I was taken captive, but several days later I was traded to a Kwahadi band for another captive who showed more promise as a wife. That was a good thing, because it would have been more difficult for me to make a place where my parents' scalps were exhibited by members of the tribe."

"I'm sorry. Have you ever thought of escaping?"

"Not since the first few months. I have mostly a good life among The People . . . that's what we call ourselves. Changes are coming. I know I can adapt. I find this an exciting time. I am hopeful I can help ease the pain for those who are not prepared for what lies ahead. The People must follow Quanah's trail. He is a great warrior, but he is an even greater leader."

"You are already helping the Kwahadi."

"At this moment, I feel very foolish. I have spoken only of myself. I have never talked about my past before today. I apologize."

"The apology is unnecessary. You know much about me from Quanah's spies. It helps if we know something of each other. I have only one question before we talk about peace terms."

"Yes?"

"You had a name in your life before the Kwahadi. What were you called?"

She hesitated. "Jael. I was known as Jael Chernik."

"Jael. I like that name. A simple one that rolls smoothly off of the tongue. Perhaps you will claim it again in your new life."

"Perhaps. I told you a small lie at our first meeting. I said I would not divulge my name because I feared my family would try to ransom me. I have no family. There is no person outside of The People who cares about what happened to Jael Chernik. My family consists of my son, Flying Crow, and me." She scrambled up from the hard ground and stood in front of him. "Now we walk, and you will tell me what you are doing to earn your fees."

Josh strolled beside the former Jael Chernik along the grassy fringes of the stream. The sun had fully risen, and he welcomed its warming rays. He described to She Who Speaks the contacts he had made with civilian authorities in his efforts to negotiate peace terms. They spent several hours talking about the specifics that should be included in any peace plan that would satisfy Quanah. He assured her again that progress was being made.

She was skeptical. "How can they be truly serious about peace when they are preparing to make war? Your Colonel Mackenzie is already assembling forces to crush the Kwahadi and our allies. Hundreds of troops are gathering along the Red River. This forces Quanah to prepare for war also. If your people are victorious, they will march the Kwahadi to the reservation, and there will be no terms but the white man's. Quanah prefers the honor of death in battle."

"I understand that. What happens on the battlefield is

beyond my control. I can only try to persuade the government people that it is in the mutual interest of the parties to hammer out a fair peace. It is difficult to persuade some that a war chief is sincere in his efforts to be a peacemaker."

"He is sincere. I promise. You must understand that Quanah is a young man of no more than twenty-six years. He is extremely intelligent and a leader with vision. He knows the years of war are numbered. Settlers are swarming like locusts over the Comanche lands. He knows that most of his lifetime, if he survives the wars, will be lived out in a different world. But how many lives are the whites willing to sacrifice before peace is forced upon the Comanche?"

"My efforts are necessarily secretive. Every decision is political. Many whites who live in the Southwest will settle for no less than the total destruction of the Kwahadi. Their representatives in Washington listen to those voices. Peace with honor and dignity does not win votes. We can only hope that wise men prevail. It happens on rare occasions."

"You should understand that Quanah is also a politician. There are those in the band who have grander titles and their own followers. Some who are older resent Quanah's influence, especially among the young warriors. He also has a serious rival, Isa-tai, who has a large following. Isa-tai is a shaman, or what some whites might call a medicine man. He claims great powers, and it is said he has ascended to the Great Spirit in the sky and returned again. He has declared that he had a vision that the Comanche will be restored to their rightful place on the plains. He is younger than Quanah, but is a squatty man who looks like an old toad. His name means 'coyote's vagina.' Very suitable in my opinion," she said contemptuously.

"You obviously are not fond of Isa-tai."

"He is an obstacle on the trail to peace and is formidable. But Quanah has been very clever in building ties with the different factions, and most know that Quanah decides when it is time for peace. It is your responsibility to bring acceptable terms to Quanah to hasten that time. In the meantime, you must understand that the Kwahadi will carry on their raids, and although Isa-tai and Quanah and others may be rivals for influence, they will be united and allied in the conduct of war."

"I will do everything I can to end the fighting."

"When you can bring a true proposal, notify Antonio at the Exchange Hotel. He will see that I get word and will convey a response. Please do not waste my time with something frivolous." She turned from him and walked away.

7

WHEN JOSH RETURNED to Santa Fe, after leaving his buckskin at the Exchange Hotel stable, he stopped by the Rivers and Sinclair office, where he was greeted by the firm's grumpy law clerk. George Hatter ruled the administration of the firm's business with an iron fist and was nearly the equivalent of another lawyer. He was an excellent draftsman and researcher and did everything legal but appear in court. Josh had given up urging the middle-aged, balding man to take the bar examination. For some reason Hatter had decided he had found his niche and was content with his lot.

George looked up from his Remington typewriter when Josh entered the office and examined his boss with obvious disdain. Josh admitted to himself he was not suitable for public inspection after several weeks in the saddle. And Hatter did not approve of the lawyer's lengthy office absences. "What brings you here?" the clerk asked with a tinge of sarcasm.

"I thought I'd check in before the office closed for the day and let you know I'm in town before I go to the Exchange Hotel to clean up. Is Danna in?"

"No, Miss Sinclair is in court. She has a breach of contract case before Judge Robinson. She has a heavy case load . . . being the only lawyer who is regularly in the office."

He ignored the clerk's little barb. "Well, I'll be here in the morning. It's after four o'clock, and I need a hot bath, a decent meal and a good night's sleep."

"Miss Sinclair said to tell you she had something very important to discuss with you. And, by the way, there is a stack of mail and messages on your desk."

"They'll wait." He wheeled and headed for the door, feeling the disapproving eyes of George Hatter burning in his back. If the little weasel disliked him so much, Josh wondered, why did he stay with the firm? He answered his own question: because Rivers and Sinclair paid him very well to manage the office. He was not indispensable, but Linda de la Cruz, although certainly carrying the raw intelligence to do the job, needed a few more years' experience before taking on the responsibility. When she was ready, watch out Hatter. When Josh left the law office, he strolled down the dusty street of the Plaza on his way to the small suite he maintained at the Exchange—a bedroom and a cramped, usually cluttered, living area. He approached the Teatro Santa Fe, the town's budding cultural center, founded and managed by his friend and occasional lover, Jessica Chandler. He wondered if she was working in the theatre and decided to find out. He tested the curved, ornate door handle. It was unlocked, so he tapped on the heavy door, before he pushed it slowly open.

"Jess," he called, as he stepped into the entranceway.

"Over here. I'll be finished in a moment."

He saw her then, on her knees in a far corner of the lobby, tapping lightly on the floor with what looked like a miniature hammer. She was wearing sandals, faded denim trousers and a baggy gray shirt, and had never looked more alluring, he thought. He noticed a short wooden bench pushed against the wall and tossed his gear on the floor and sat down, content to follow the sway of her butt as she worked at whatever she was doing. Finally, she got up and turned and faced him.

"You stink," she said. "I can smell you from here. Stale sweat, horseshit, and a mix of other revolting odors."

"And I'm glad to see you, too," he replied.

She brushed her soft, black hair away from her forehead. "What do you think?"

"About what?"

She stepped back and extended her open hand as though presenting a guest speaker. "The floor."

"The floor?"

"It's new, you idiot. I just set the last tile."

"Oh, sure." He studied the floor, nodding his head approvingly. "Very nice. I like brown. Brown's good."

She placed her hands on her hips, and he could see her green eyes starting to spark. "The color is terra cotta. You make your living with words, and the best you can come up with is 'brown?'"

"Sorry, that's what I meant to say. 'Terra cotta.'"

"Liar."

"Forgive me. You have made some impressive improvements." He cast his eyes about the room and realized she had re-plastered the walls and had been putting a lot of work into dressing up the building, which had been a small, abandoned Catholic church. There had been several performances there since Jessica arrived with him in Santa Fe the previous fall. She had adapted the raised pulpit area as a stage and kept the existing pews for seating. Jessica, an experienced actress, performed the lead female roles and recruited local would-be thespians for other parts. These actors appeared for whatever satisfaction they received from performing, which enhanced profits. This appealed to Josh because he had invested for a ten percent share in the enterprise.

"You're making progress," she said. "I'm saving money by doing most of the work myself."

"That, I do like."

"The Bella Union Theatre Ballet is going to perform here in July, you know."

"Ballet?"

"From San Francisco. They've committed to four days. They're on tour. We're the next stop after Denver."

"Who will attend?"

"The place will be packed. And you will attend, if you know what's good for you."

"Peace offering. Let me take you to dinner at La Castillo this evening."

"You'll take a bath?"

"I promise."

8

JESSICA'S NAKED BODY clung to Josh's like a magnet, one long leg draped over his thigh, arm flung across his waist and her long, black hair splayed over his chest, where her head nestled. He had awakened when he thought he heard steps in the hallway outside his suite, which afforded access to all of the rooms that lined it. The sound of folks walking would not have been so unusual a few hours after midnight. Strangely, it was the stealth of the movement that had alerted him. Too many days in Comanche land, he thought. Nonetheless, he listened.

Jessica seemed to be sleeping the sleep of the dead. He could feel the gentle rise and fall of her breasts against his ribs. She had been finally sated but had ridden him to near exhaustion after they returned to his rooms, which were at the opposite end of the long hallway from hers. This second floor of the hotel housed mostly full-time residents, and their proximity was convenient for their occasional wild coupling, but they were more friends than lovers, and their stolen moments in one of their rooms were essentially to satisfy a hunger they mutually recognized in each other.

Jessica, in her mid-thirties, was some half dozen years older than Josh and had made clear she was not seeking a mate, in the matrimonial sense. She had been married to her acting mentor, a man twenty years her senior, for many years before he was savagely murdered during a Comanche attack on their small theatrical troupe, which had foolishly ventured upon the Staked Plains. Josh had come upon the scene and intervened to liberate Jessica from the attackers. She had endured widowhood well, mourning her late husband for all of a day before she crawled into Josh's bedroll. To Josh's embarrassment this had led to the both of them being captured naked at sunrise by Quanah and a small war party. It was during their captivity that he met She Who Speaks and negotiated for Jessica's release as a part of his bargain for ransom of Erin McKenna and his agreement to represent Quanah. This common experience had forged their bond.

He heard the footsteps in the hallway again and, then, someone tinkering with the door lock. He gently eased away from Jessica's clinging body and quietly got out of bed. She rolled over, clutched her pillow and seemed not to notice his absence, as he slipped into his cotton undershorts and reached for his Colt, which was nestled in its holster on the bed stand. He moved stealthily from the bedroom to the hallway door. Then, just before he slid back the deadbolt, an envelope slipped under the door and he heard light footsteps racing down the hall. He opened the door and stepped out into the hazy light of the few oil lamps that lit the hallway in time to catch a glimpse of a gangly, barefoot Mexican boy turning the corner that led to the stairway.

He shrugged and returned to his suite, stooping to pick up

the envelope. It was unsealed, and he plucked a small sheet of thick, unlined parchment paper from it. He walked over to the little two-chair table that served as his desk and dining set. He lit the kerosene lamp, turning it up just enough to allow him to read the message. The writing was something of a scrawl, probably intentionally so, he thought. It was a short, simple note: *Meet Quanah's contact in St. Mary's sanctuary at sundown. Tomorrow night. Important.*

He flipped the message onto the table and turned off the lamp. He needed to sleep on this. Damn, he was tired. He returned to the bedroom and climbed back into bed and collapsed on the straw mattress. Jessica stirred and rolled toward him. He froze, turning very still.

"Josh," she murmured.

He feigned sleep. He felt her fingers gently raking his curly chest hair.

"I'd better go to my room. One more time?"

"I don't think I can," he said groggily.

She snuggled up to him, and he could feel a taut nipple brushing his skin. Her fingers danced down his belly and inched beneath his undershorts. "I guess I can," he said, rising to the occasion.

9

JOSH TOOK A chair in front of Danna's desk, and set his coffee mug on a leather coaster she kept there for the desktop's protection. Sometimes she was disgustingly tidy. He thought the interconnecting watermarks on his own desk gave it character.

"You look tired," Danna remarked. "Rough night?"

Did he detect a knowing smirk on her lips? "Yes, I'm tired. I've spent several weeks on the Staked Plains, taken a bullet in my shoulder, and slept with one eye open all that time. Damn right, I'm tired," he said irritably.

"A bullet?"

"Somebody ambushed me. Not Comanche. They saved my hide. She Who Speaks patched me up. It was a flesh wound high on my left shoulder." He rubbed the spot gingerly, although there was no lingering pain.

"She Who Speaks? That's the woman who interprets for Quanah."

"Yes, and she's sort of a secret counselor to him as well. I think she's more influential than most of the Kwahadi are aware. Very intelligent. She was known as Jael Chernik when she was taken captive at age fourteen. Speaks four or five languages fluently."

"Interesting woman."

"Yes, she'd make a hell of a good lawyer. I guess, in a way, she's already lawyering for Quanah . . . speaking of which, this was pushed under my door last night." He plucked the note from his coat pocket and handed it to Danna.

She studied it for a moment, and then she looked up and seemed to be scrutinizing him with her penetrating blue eyes. "Don't even think about it. Don't you have a contact for Quanah?"

"Yes, but I haven't seen him since I've been back. And he does prefer privacy when we talk. He came to my room the last time we spoke."

"So why doesn't he just come to your room again?"

"I don't know. Maybe I'll find out tonight."

"I don't like it. You said you've already been ambushed once. This could be a set up. St. Mary's is a pretty remote place."

"If it's an ambush, this time I won't be caught by surprise." He changed the subject. "Hatter said you had something important to talk to me about."

"Several things, actually. The first has to do with operation of the office. We need another lawyer . . . two more would be nice, unless you plan to spend more time here in the near future. We could handle the lawyers without additional staff, and I'm certain we could find someone who would work for a share of his or her gross billings . . . it would be no risk for us income-wise."

"We're doing well. I can't argue that, and I know you're overworked. You've created something close to order out of chaos since you joined me in the practice."

"I just think there are great opportunities to grow the firm, and we should be taking advantage of them."

"So, who did you hire?"

Her Nordic complexion flushed with crimson. "Well, I didn't hire him yet, but I told him there was a possibility. I told him, as senior partner, you had the last word."

"Tell me about him."

"His name is Martin Locke . . . goes by Marty. Confederate veteran. Virginia law school graduate."

"Your school. Did you know him there?"

"No, he's about your age and must have finished a few years before I enrolled. He practiced with a small firm in southern Virginia before he withdrew from the partnership and came west with a wagon train."

"Why did he leave the other firm?"

"His wife and daughter died during childbirth. He says he headed west to escape the ghosts . . . but it hasn't worked. He decided it was time to quit running, and he thought Santa Fe was as good a place as any to stop."

"You can't escape the ghosts."

"No, but you can learn to deal with them. Remember, I have my ghosts, too. I saw my parents and little brother murdered by Comanchero. I won't ever forget it. But the ghosts remind me that I am fortunate to be alive and that I have memories of times and people that gave me joy. My ghosts are a part of whatever I have become. I ran for years from the ghosts, but once I learned to embrace them, life got better."

"Sounds like something the former Jael Chernik might say. Anyway, go ahead and work out a deal with this Marty."

"Not until you meet him. We're having dinner with him

tomorrow evening at La Castillo."

"I just ate there last night."

"I know."

"You do?"

"I do."

That pretty well confirmed she knew the generalities about the remainder of his evening as well. "You said there was something else we needed to talk about . . . something important."

"This is more difficult. It's about your son . . . Michael."

Josh leaned forward in his chair, a shiver of apprehension racing down his back. "What about Michael?"

"It's not bad news. I just don't know what to make of it."

"Spit it out. Please."

Danna told him about her meeting with Clayborne Pierce and the man's proposal to ransom Michael. She explained the necessary financial arrangements in detail while Josh listened intently. She could feel the tension and seething anger build as she spoke.

"Where is the son of a bitch?" Josh asked. "I want to talk to him . . . in a way he'll understand."

"I have no idea. I'm sure he knows you've returned, and I suspect he'll make an appearance in the next few days. As I indicated, he was concerned about your reaction and wants to give you time to cool down and think about what he is proposing."

Josh glowered at her.

"Don't look at me like that. I'm the messenger."

"I realize that, but I don't think much of these bastards that make money off of human misery."

"We make some money off of human misery, too. Death, divorce, family feuds. Nobody comes to a lawyer for a laugh. We help solve their problems and get paid for it."

"You sound like Pierce's lawyer right now."

"I'm sorry, Josh. But if you want your son back, I suggest you think of this as a business deal. What about the money?"

"Pierce's fees, I can handle. I assume we have enough in firm funds for me to draw against my share for that."

"That shouldn't be a problem."

"Ransom would be another matter. After I talk to this Clayborne Pierce, I'll send word to Dad. He might be able to help, if necessary."

10

St. Mary's sat in the foothills not more than a mile northwest of Santa Fe, set back some fifty yards from a narrow, dusty trail that led to nowhere in particular. The small adobe church was maintained by the Catholic Church as an outpost of sorts. Mass was conducted monthly or upon request of one of the scattered local Mexican farmers for a funeral, wedding or baptism for someone who still claimed a traditional connection with the church. The church did not have its own priest, but members of one of the Catholic Orders rotated duties to provide for the occasional services.

Josh had been surveying the church and grounds for nearly half an hour from his perch on a mound of rock rising from the rugged terrain on the opposite side of the trail. When he arrived, a sorrel mare and sleepy donkey were hitched to the rail in front of the church, a strange combination, he thought. He assumed his contact was waiting inside the church, but why two animals? And he worried about the outbuildings behind the church. What he assumed was a former rectory nearest the church proper was crumbling into oblivion and offered no shelter, but the remnants of a roofless adobe barn could hide three or four men and horses with ease.

It was nearly sundown and a time for choosing. He slid down the backside of the slope, got up and crept over to the buckskin he had tethered and left grazing the sparse, dry grass that wedged its way between the rocks. He pulled his Winchester from its scabbard and started walking toward St. Mary's. Out of habit, he caressed the Army Colt at his side.

When he reached the church door, he stopped and pondered what might lay behind it. His church visits were infrequent. Levi Rivers had assured his children they were all baptized Methodists and ready to meet their maker, but there was not a church within twenty miles of the Slash R in remote northeastern New Mexico. Their mother, Auralie, had read to the family daily from the Bible, so he was not ignorant of things religious. He just did not know much about church structures. His adult proximity to such structures had not improved his attendance. Of course, Santa Fe had no surplus of things Protestant. The Catholic churches he had observed at the occasional funeral generally included a vestibule inside the entrance—just like Jessica's theatre—and a sanctuary, at the rear of which was a door through which the priest and other ritualistic participants entered and departed. He assumed this was some type of preparation area. It was likely St. Mary's conformed to the pattern, he decided. But the door at the rear concerned him.

He pulled his Colt from its holster and slowly opened the door. He would not surprise anyone, for the thick, sagging door creaked loudly on rusty hinges. He cast his eyes about the sanctuary which was laid out with a center aisle and rows of pews lining each side, and, as he had guessed, the closed mystery door off to the speaker's right side behind the pulpit. To his left, on her knees, near the wall in front of the second pew was a nun, her hands meeting in prayer. That would explain the donkey, he supposed. But where was the horse's rider?

The nun was problematic if this was an ambush. He also considered the possibility that the nun was not a nun, but the person he was to meet—or a hired killer. He pondered the questions for only a moment when the door behind the pulpit opened. Out of the door came walking a short, stocky man with hands tied behind his back and a thin rawhide rope looped in a hangman's knot drawn snugly about his neck and held taut by someone behind the door. The young Mexican's eyes were wide with terror and fastened pleadingly on Josh's.

A deep voice from behind the door called, "Rivers, throw your gun up front where I can see it, or I put a hole in the back of this greaser's head."

"I don't think so."

"We just want to talk."

We? That could mean there were two of them behind that door. "You didn't have to go through all of this to have a chat. I'm sure you know where my office is. Let this man go and then we'll talk."

He eased the Army Colt out of its holster just as he heard the door creak behind him. He turned toward the door, and suddenly a deafening explosion filled the sanctuary. The door from the vestibule flew open, and a huge, bear-like man stepped in, his pistol ready. Josh heard two quick gunshots from the front of the sanctuary but focused on the new intruder. "Drop it," he said.

The man did not, and Josh fired twice and sent two bullets tearing into the big man's chest. The gunslinger stared at him in disbelief and then looked down at the blood starting to trickle from his wounds, before his legs gave way and he slumped to the floor. Josh swung around, his gun ready, but saw instantly that the weapon wasn't needed. The young Mexican was sprawled on the floor, the back of his skull obliterated by what was obviously a shotgun blast. Another man lay nearby, apparently the bearer of the shotgun.

He looked toward the nun, who stood at the far end of her pew, the pistol in her hand still showing a haze of smoke. "Thanks," he said, "but—" Then he recognized his tall partner.

"You're welcome," Danna said, pushing back her cowl. She moved toward the pulpit. "The bastard shot the young man before I could do anything. It all happened so fast."

Josh joined her at the front of the sanctuary. He shook his head in disbelief. "Maybe I should have dropped my gun. Antonio might still be alive."

"You would both be dead. I probably would be, too. Nun or not, they couldn't leave witnesses. You knew the young man?"

"He was our contact with Quanah."

"So it's no coincidence that Antonio was the victim. Do you have another contact?"

"No, but Quanah's people are very resourceful. When they're unable to establish communications with Antonio, they'll find another way to reach me. I'm a little concerned I couldn't send a message Quanah's direction right now, but it will likely be several months before I need to. What bothers me most is that someone knows that Antonio was our contact. Killing him was some kind of message, I suppose. But they obviously intended to kill me as well. Whoever hired these men want to break our link to Quanah. It's obviously the same man . . . or men . . . who wanted to see me killed out on the Staked Plains. Somebody is aware that we are working with Quanah, and, for some reason he has a huge stake in stopping our efforts. I suspect Oliver McKenna, but I can't prove it. And I can't figure out why it's so important."

"What do we do about this mess?"

"I'll visit the U.S. Marshal tomorrow morning and tell him my version of what happened here, and he can investigate and get the bodies removed."

"Your version?"

"Yes, for one thing you weren't here. How would we explain your presence? What are you doing here anyway and how'd you get so damn good with a gun?"

"Answering your first question, the note was an obvious set-up, and I'm not ready to lose my law partner yet."

"Yet?"

"Yet. It's more or less inevitable I lose you sooner or later given the life you've chosen. Anyway, I thought you might need some back-up. Your friend, Jessica, dug out my nun's habit from her costume wardrobe, and I rented Pedro out there from the livery. Now your second question. My father taught me how to fire a rifle when I was eight years old, and after he was murdered, I made it my business to learn to fire every kind of gun that might be helpful in protecting me. I have no interest in being a victim."

"Well, Sister Danna, we'd better get out of here. I'm not going to ride your donkey, but Buck won't mind if I walk with you . . . unless you want to race."

11

La Castillo was a poor excuse for a castle, Josh thought, but the food was good enough for a king. From the outside, a customer was lured by a single, crumbling spire, all of a dozen feet in height, which erupted from the flat rooftop of the compact building and leaned toward the front like a rhinoceros horn. The plastered interior walls were bare and pocked, and the dining area was cramped and packed with patrons.

Danna and Martin Locke were taking advantage of the vast Mexican menu offered by the restaurant, but Josh had downed a bit too much of that a couple nights ago and was sticking with steak and fried potatoes. According to Danna and Locke, the red wine was excellent, and Josh sipped at it agreeably, although he had never been able to discern much difference in wines. He would have preferred a sarsaparilla.

He found Locke to be an interesting man, intelligent and easy to engage in conversation. Locke was nearly as tall as Josh, with thick, short-cropped black hair and steel-gray eyes that always seemed to be probing for something. Women no doubt found him handsome, and his mellow Virginia drawl had a seductive quality to it.

"You mentioned your father was a lawyer," Josh said. "Where did he practice?"

"Williamsburg. Mostly real estate and probate. I have a preference for the courtroom. I probably would have joined Dad's practice, though, if he hadn't died at Gettysburg. He was an infantry colonel, the quietest, most peaceful man you could imagine. Ironic that he died at war."

"A lot of ironies come out of war. I'm sorry. Any other family?"

"None in Virginia. My mother died when I was ten, and before that I lost a little sister to smallpox. I have an uncle, Myles Locke, who practices law in Manhattan, Kansas, a little town not far from Fort Riley. He has a son, Cameron, who practices with him. Cam attended school at Virginia when the war broke out and joined the Confederate army, and we spent some time together during the war years. Cam's twin is a lawyer in Nebraska . . . he fought for the North . . . a Medal of Honor recipient."

"Marty, Danna told me about your personal loss, and I empathize, I assure you."

"I know. You've dealt with your own loss."

"Danna thinks you're a good fit for our firm."

Danna remained silent but nodded her agreement.

Josh continued. "I agree. Danna wants to focus on commercial and real estate law, and you like the courtroom. That would make a good match. I'm more of a generalist . . . and I'm out of the office a lot."

"I understand."

"My only concern is whether you are committed to a future

in Santa Fe. Danna and I have agreed that, after a year's trial period, we would be able to offer a phase-in to partnership. But, if we're going to take on another lawyer, I want someone who sees our office as more than a stopover."

"I love this place," Locke said. "It's so completely different from the life I lived before. It's the perfect place for a new beginning. You won't be sorry you took me on. And I'll have to let you find out for yourself, but my word is good."

"Then I'll see you at the office in the morning."

"And I've set up your first appointment," Danna said.

Locke raised his brow in surprise. "Seriously?"

"Seriously. His name is William Bonney. He's about fifteen years old."

12

TABITHA RIVERS WAS impatient for a story, as she straddled the smoke-gray gelding—Smokey—she had confiscated from her father's Slash R ranch when she took up residence in Santa Fe. She had been in the saddle for eight days with the fifty-man detachment out of Fort Union. Her butt was sore as a toothache, and she would die for a bath, but damned if any of the soldiers would hear a complaint. She had dispatched several mundane stories of life on the march with a military courier. Unfortunately, her editors at *The Santa Fe New Mexican* would soon shove these to the back page if she didn't come up with some blood and gore. Unfortunately, that's what sold papers; it always had and always would, she supposed.

It was about an hour short of noon, she guessed, as they rode deeper into northern Texas, following the course of the Canadian River. It was only late May, but it might as well have been July. The sun was bearing down like a fiery kiln, and her cotton shirt was already sweat-soaked. She knew she stunk, just like everybody else in the column. She tugged her wide-brimmed Plainsman hat down over her forehead to block some of the sun's glare, nearly covering her shorn hair, and then she saw the smoke. Lieutenant Kelly must have seen it, too, because he signaled the column to a halt, and then, with one of his Tonkawa scouts, galloped his horse a short distance away from the troops. He pulled his binoculars from his saddlebags and raised them to his eyes. He seemed to be scrutinizing something on the eastern horizon.

She wondered if he would recognize what he was seeing. She liked Sean Kelly well enough. He was a few years older than she, but she looked upon him as something of a child. Fresh from West Point with his Second Lieutenant's commission, he had grown up in Boston and never had been west of the Mississippi until his orders sent him to Fort Union. He was fair-haired and handsome in a baby-faced sort of way, and when his greenhorn days had passed, she suspected she might find him interesting. For now, though, she often found his naiveté annoying.

Tabby edged her horse forward past some of the enlisted cavalry so she could listen to the exchange between the lieutenant and his sergeants. Momentarily, he rode back to the column with his Tonkawa scout.

"There's smoke in the southwest," Lieutenant Kelly announced, stating the obvious.

Very astute. And it required field glasses to figure that out?

"I'm sending Rattlesnake and White Wolf to scout it out. We'll follow not far behind."

Tabby suddenly had to pee, and she wheeled Smokey away from the column, spotted, a lonely clump of sagebrush and nudged the gelding toward it and dismounted. She quickly pulled down her britches and relieved herself behind the scant cover, knowing half the men in Company Two were furtively eyeing her backside. She was well past worrying about that. She had left her modesty in Santa Fe. She guessed it was occasionally uncomfortable for male soldiers to take care of bodily functions with a woman nearby, as well.

She quickly caught up with the troopers and reined in near the front of the column again. The lieutenant caught sight of her and slowed his mount as she edged closer.

"This could be trouble," he said.

"It's not a prairie fire. The smoke's too concentrated and not moving anywhere. Too much of it for a campfire. I'd bet on Comanche mischief . . . or they're trying to suck us into a trap."

"A trap?"

"Not too likely. But we're not going to surprise anybody. They know where we're at, and there won't be any Comanche there when we get to the source of the fire."

"You make them sound like ghosts or something."

"I'd rather deal with a ghost."

They rode in silence for some time, and, soon, the pungent scent of smoke drifted in with the dry wind and stung her nostrils. Her eyes started to tear, just as she caught sight of the Tonkawa scouts racing their mounts toward the column. Lieutenant Kelly rode out to meet them, and in a few moments, he was engaged in animated conversation with Rattlesnake. She knew that the scrawny Tonkawa spoke a smattering of English and filled in the lapses with sign language, which the lieutenant was surprisingly adept at. White Wolf, on the other hand, rarely spoke to anyone other than Rattlesnake, but Tabby thought his dark eyes reflected a keen intelligence, and she sensed that his partner tended to defer to White Wolf's opinions more often than not. Certainly, White Wolf, a muscular young man who was taller than most Tonkawa males, was the superior horseman. He rides like a Comanche, she thought.

Momentarily, Lieutenant Kelly returned, and Tabby listened intently while he spoke to his sergeants. "It's a settler's house," he said. "Comanche, of course. The scouts didn't ride in, but Rattlesnake said there were no signs of life. We need to check it out. Order the bugler to sound 'Boots and Saddles.'"

13

As the column neared the smoking farm buildings, Tabitha Rivers was pulled back to a day she had pushed out of her mind for several years. She recalled now that bright spring morning when the Comanche raided the Slash R. Her father and brothers and all but a few cowhands were some miles away from the home place, rounding up cattle. They were to be gone for several more days, castrating the young bull calves and branding any critter in the herds that didn't already carry someone else's brand. Tabby had been collecting eggs from the nests in the henhouse, and Mom was baking in the kitchen. Cassie would have been in the parlor nursing little Michael.

The first clue of trouble came from old Luke, whose arthritis kept him at headquarters tending to whatever chores Tabby's mother might toss his way. He and two green hands also stayed back to provide a skeleton crew for guard duty, although there had not been any Indian raids that deep into northeastern New Mexico for several years. "To the house," yelled the grizzled cowhand, "Indians. Get to the house."

The thick adobe walls of the house with their narrow

windows made the ranch house a veritable fortress, but it was too late. Tabby had stepped out of the henhouse just as the first shots were fired. She saw Luke in the yard with his Winchester firing at a dozen or more Indians sweeping like a Texas tornado into the ranch yard. In a matter of seconds Luke had been impaled on a Comanche lance, and the other two hands, who had come running from the bunkhouse, were quickly pin cushions for Comanche arrows. Three or four of the warriors had dismounted and raced into the house, and Tabby shivered as she heard the screams in her memory. It was only later she had learned of the rape and mutilation of Cassie and Aurelie Rivers.

Tabby's rifle was in the house, so she hid in the henhouse until the fires started. Then she stumbled through the smoke and to the open doorway, where she was met by a fierce-looking painted warrior. She remembered a stone-headed war club arcing toward her head.

It was nightfall before she awakened, her head racked by pain and her mind disoriented. Something struck her ribs harshly several times, and she looked up to see the face of her captor. Only then did she realize her clothes had been torn away and that she lay naked on the grass. The Comanche pushed his breechclout off to one side and knelt down next to her, leaving no doubt what he intended. She started to roll away, and the warrior grabbed her arm and yanked her back before hammering her nose several times with his fist. When he mounted her, she did not resist.

It was over quickly, but several hours later he visited again and repeated the rape. This time he left a blanket behind, and she gratefully snatched it up and wrapped it snuggly about her shoulders. She sat in silence trying to appraise her dilemma. She had heard the tales of Comanche captives. Had she been claimed as this man's wife? Perhaps, that was why she had not been raped by others.

The night air was more balmy than cool, and, with her blanket cover, Tabby was not particularly uncomfortable. The agony in her skull had abated significantly, and her fingers softly and tentatively traced the wound on the side of her head. She probed the egg-size lump there and felt the stickiness of the matted blood. The soreness between her thighs was a mere annoyance in comparison to the head wound. Her mind was consumed by two thoughts: survival and escape. She reminded herself she had to do the former to accomplish the latter.

She surveyed her surroundings. A full moon afforded some light, but she was hidden away in a little arbor of shrubs and scrub trees of some kind just off a larger clearing where no more than five warriors were squatted around the fading coals of a fire, engaged in what she took to be a minor argument of some kind. She suspected the dialogue might determine her future or lack of one. Her warrior—strange that she was thinking of him as *her* warrior—was the most vocal, and she had a sense he was staking his exclusive claim on her. The others were more interested in shared bounty. This band would be less than half the number who raided the ranch. There was no sign of Michael, who would not have been silent unless he was dead. She shuddered at that thought. It was more likely the raiding party had split up and that Michael had been taken by the other band. That was the best she could hope for. As for her mother and Cassie, she had no doubt about their fate. She prayed they had not suffered long.

She tore her mind away from memories of the raid, studying the landscape around her. Beyond the dying embers of the fire, she could make out the ribbon of a river. It had to be the Canadian. Unless she had slept for two days, there would not be another creek or river of this size within a day's ride of the Slash R. She focused on the river. It would lead her home if she followed it upstream toward the northwest, for the river's course carved its way through a corner of the Slash R's thirty thousand acre spread. But even if she escaped the camp and followed the river's path, the Comanche would track her easily, and, when she was recaptured, the option of being a Comanche squaw would likely be foreclosed. On the other hand, her father, Levi Rivers, often bragged that his tomboy daughter could swim like a fish.

She watched while the warriors, one by one, moved away from the fire and spread out their buffalo robes on the ground. Her warrior picked up his own robe and moved toward the arbor. He spread out the robe beside her and motioned for her to lie on it. She complied. He quickly took her again, before he rolled off her body and collapsed on the robe next to her. She lay motionless for some minutes before she heard his soft, rhythmic snoring. She slowly inched over onto her side and then stopped to listen. He still slept. She had always heard that Indians awakened at the hum of a mosquito, but this guy seemed to be sleeping the sleep of a dead drunk. Busy day. Busy night. Her eyes scrutinized the arbor, trying to ferret out a weapon. Obviously, the warrior was no fool. His scalping knife and any other weapons were evidently on his side of the robe. That choice saved his life.

Tabby rose, planning to sign her need to slip away to pee if he woke. She crept from the arbor and into the campfire clearing. She had thought of trying to sneak through the brush and saplings to the river but was certain the warriors would hear her movement. So she just raced through the camp like a deer, making a beeline for the river. She slipped quietly into the icy water, the river running full now from mountain snow melt, and, without looking back, began to swim against the slow-moving current.

14

THE COLUMN MOVED out at a slow trot after spending the better part of a day and most of the next morning at the burnt-out settlers' cabin. The bodies discovered at the farmstead were both male. From what remained of him it appeared that the older man must have been in his late forties. He had been staked out on the prairie and his genitals carved out, leaving a bloody cavern in his crotch. Hot coals still smoldered on his stomach, where the raiders had built a fire. Tabitha feared his torment had not been brief.

The other body was that of a boy, no more than sixteen, found near the small corral. Arrows lodged in his throat and chest suggested he had been killed before his scalping, and his corpse was not otherwise maimed. He likely had a rifle that had been taken by the Comanche.

While the soldiers buried the dead and salvaged any personal belongings that might identify the dead, Rattlesnake and White Wolf paced the ground around the farmstead proper. When they were satisfied they had unraveled the story in the signs there, Rattlesnake reported it was their belief that a woman and a small girl also resided on the farm. This was confirmed by remnants of clothing scattered about the place. There were Kiowa signs as well, he observed.

The scouts then departed and didn't return until the next morning just as the troops were preparing to saddle up. Rattlesnake informed Lieutenant Kelly that the raiding party was exceptionally large for an attack on a single family—as many as fifty warriors. He surmised that this hapless family simply had the misfortune to be in the path of a larger movement of Comanche and Kiowa heading for a rendezvous somewhere south, likely in Red River country. The party had split up some ten miles southeast of the farm, one group heading due south and the other riding southwesterly. Rattlesnake thought this was a ruse to confuse any pursuers who might be hoping to rescue the woman and her daughter, forcing the searchers to also split forces or to make a hard choice. In either case, the Tonkawa insisted, a trap was being set, and Company Two would be providing the rabbits.

This left Lieutenant Kelly in a quandary. His orders were to meet up at Adobe Walls, a trading post located some fifty miles northeasterly on the Canadian, with cavalry units out of Fort Sill. The troops were expected to be under the command of Colonel Ranald Mackenzie. From there the lieutenant understood the army would be moving south toward the Red River in the same direction the raiders were headed. Tabitha could see that Kelly was itching to follow the abductors, but, fortunately, he was a West Pointer, who intended to be career military, and he had the good sense not to abort his fledgling career by treacherous heroics. He decided to send a courier ahead to inform the officers gathering their commands at Adobe Walls that the Fort Union troops could be expected to arrive within two days' time. He allowed Tabitha to send her stories with the courier who would, hopefully, put them in the hands of someone who would eventually carry her words on to *The New Mexican*.

15

JOSH STEPPED OUT of the Exchange Hotel onto the boardwalk that stretched down the front of the expansive adobe building, shaded from the sun's glare by the portales that reached out to the street and stretched the length of the hotel. He turned and walked slowly along the edge of San Francisco Street that adjoined the hotel, his eyes alert, his right hand swinging within easy reach of his Colt. After the recent attempts on his life, he did not take his safety for granted anywhere.

He had just lunched with Martin Locke and Danna in the open-air *placita* that afforded pleasant dining within the walls of the Exchange. Marty had told his new partners about his encounter with young William Bonney, who had previously been employed as a dishwasher by the manager of the Exchange's dining room. Bonney had been discharged for being quarrelsome with the other help and disrespectful of the manager. Bonney had insisted the allegations were false, but he had been planning to leave Santa Fe and head for southern New Mexico anyway, and he was owed forty dollars back wages, which the manager had refused to pay. Bonney had told Marty matter-of-factly that he preferred not to kill the manager and that he would pay Marty ten dollars if he would collect the amount due.

"This kid's blue eyes are like ice," Marty had said. "I think the manager's tinkering with his own life if he doesn't pay up. Obviously, we can't convey Bonney's threat, but I'll have a talk with the manager after we're finished here and see if I can take care of it. I'm eagerly awaiting my next complicated case."

Danna had assured him that she had an accused murderer for him to defend. "He's probably guilty of killing the man," she said, "but there's a self-defense argument, I suppose, although it's complicated by the fact our client was trying to rob the victim's jewelry store. You'll have more than your share of these for now. For a city of four thousand souls, we keep the two undertakers unusually busy . . . as well as the courts. Anyway, I'm done as a criminal lawyer. The civil practice isn't giving me any time for dealing with the accused lawbreakers."

Marty seemed willing to take any case that came his way for now, so Josh was glad to be rid of the small bit of guilt he carried for leaving all the work to Danna when he was traveling on one of his missions. He knew Danna was not all that fond of trial work, and she had an organized mind and tolerance for solitude that made her a natural for dealing with business issues and the complicated real estate laws that had to be reconciled with the old Spanish land grants in the territory. Marty seemed more likely to take to the courtroom side of the practice, so he decided he had prospects of a good tandem.

His errand now had been triggered by a message, for some unknown reason, delivered to Danna by a small Mexican boy that morning. The message was from Clayborne Pierce and included instructions for Josh to meet the man who called himself a "private searcher," at the Exchange Hotel's stables at one o'clock sharp. The location had seemed strange. Why not just meet in the privacy of Josh's office? It made him a little wary. Another setup? Danna did not think so. She speculated that the man didn't want to give Josh a turf edge. Marty had offered to join him, but Josh did not want to scare Pierce off.

When Josh turned into the multi-rowed stable, he caught sight of a lean man, who matched Danna's description of Pierce, leaning against the gate to Buck's stall.

"Mr. Pierce?" he asked, as he approached.

Pierce stepped away from the gate and extended his hand, and Josh reluctantly accepted it with his own. The man had a firm grip and met Josh's eyes unflinchingly, he noted.

"Mr. Rivers . . . may I call you 'Josh'?"

"That's fine."

"I'm Clay. I assume Miss Sinclair has explained what I'm proposing?"

"Yes, and I must say the idea of your holding my son for ransom doesn't set well with me."

"I thought that might be the case. That's why I wanted to let the idea settle a bit before we spoke. Look at this from my standpoint. This is my business . . . the way I make a living. I don't have the inclination to risk my life rescuing captive children or wives for the sake of charity. I have certain skills, and this is the way I've chosen to use them. I would suggest that some things lawyers have to do don't always look so noble from the public's perspective."

Josh shrugged. He couldn't argue that point. "So, let's talk business. You know where my son's at?"

"No, I do not. But my Tonkawa associate is quite certain he

knows. We have an understanding. He does not tell me the location until he makes final confirmation and I have contracted with the family. That way, in case someone would try to use extreme measures to force the information from me, it would be pointless, because I don't have it."

"I see. How do I know this isn't some kind of hoax?"

Pierce withdrew a folded sheet of paper from his coat pocket and unfolded it and handed the crisp sheet to Josh. "This is a list of people I have helped. Several live within fifteen miles of Santa Fe. Check with them and see what they think about my services. I am a man of my word, Josh. And I am smart enough to know that if I attempted to defraud you, I would pay a dear price . . . perhaps even my life."

"Then we do understand each other." Josh said softly. He reached into his front trouser pocket and fished out a roll of bills. "One thousand dollars. You get another thousand when you negotiate the ransom and a final thousand upon Michael's return. If you cannot locate him, first payment gets refunded. I have already drafted an escrow agreement for the bank. You may stop by my office and sign it and accompany my secretary to the bank with the money, if you wish."

"I'll sign, but I will trust you to deposit the funds."

"How long before we hear from you?"

"It may be as long as a month. But I will report as soon as I have verified your son's location and made a deal with the Comanche."

"Will there be trouble making a deal?"

"I have never failed to come to terms. I have had several families who could not raise the funds. The Comanche will likely want gold coinage, possibly in Mexican dollars. It has been easier to reach an agreement the past few years with the end of the Comanche wars in sight. They know if they don't get a price for the captives, the white women and children will likely be repatriated without compensation on the reservation."

"I'll look to hear from you within a month then. If I'm not in Santa Fe when you return, you may speak with Miss Sinclair. She will have authority to proceed with arrangements for any ransom."

16

JOSH SAT IN a tattered buffalo hide-covered chair in the single room of the clapboard building that served as Dr. Jacob Sturm's office, examining room, clinic and hospital. The structure was set off a half mile west of Fort Sill proper, and Josh was unclear whether the medical facility was sponsored by the army or by the Quakers, who operated an Indian school no more than fifty paces down the road. The three beds were occupied by two ancient, frail Indians, who appeared not far from meeting up with the Great Spirit, and a young soldier, whose scarlet and sweat-soaked face and neck indicated a raging fever. Josh knew the man was military because of the rumpled uniform that was tossed haphazardly over a chair next to his bed.

A young, blonde woman, with a bright smile that seemed out of place in the gloomy environment, entered the room, which was about fifteen feet wide by thirty feet long. She carried a tin pail of water and some rags and headed directly toward the soldier, calling over her shoulder, "Doctor Sturm will be here shortly."

Josh watched as the cheery woman began to bathe the

soldier's face and neck, humming a familiar but unidentifiable tune, as her fingers danced the wet cotton cloths over his burning skin. No privacy here, he thought. No curtains to separate the patients. Surgery performed on the rickety operating table would play to an audience, most of whom apparently would not have much interest, though.

The army maintained an infirmary of sorts within the fort boundaries, so Josh was a bit curious about Sturm's facility. He had heard that Dr. Sturm was essentially a self-anointed physician, which was not all that uncommon in the West. He knew that the man, married to a Caddo woman, occasionally served as a scout for the army, had passable fluency in several native languages, and was frequently hired on as an interpreter for peace conferences with the tribes. He was also looked upon by some in the Bureau of Indian Affairs as something of an expert in the field of army and Indian relations. In particular he had the ear and respect of Colonel Ranald Slidell Mackenzie, known among many of the Indians of the southern plains as the No Finger Chief or Bad Hand, because of disfiguring Civil War injuries to his hand. Mackenzie, in turn, had the ear of President Ulysses S. Grant.

Josh's contacts had informed him that Sturm was the man to know if he wanted to hammer out favorable peace terms for Quanah. Time was running out. He needed a breakthrough.

The door opened again, and a scruffy-looking man with a short-cropped beard and deeply receding hairline walked in. Josh stood, but the wiry man seemed preoccupied and did not notice him at first. Then, when he saw Josh, the man looked at his visitor quizzically. Josh stepped forward and offered his hand. "Josh Rivers, Dr. Sturm. I'm a lawyer from Santa Fe. I represent

Quanah of the Kwahadi Comanche."

As Josh suspected, the last statement caught Sturm's attention. Now he could see the man was studying him with some interest.

"Pull your chair up to my desk, Mr. Rivers. I'm always interested in anything to do with Quanah." Sturm moved around the desk and took a seat in a wobbly chair. He nodded, which Josh took as a signal to tell his story.

The man's pale blue eyes were bloodshot, and his skin burnt brown and dry by the sun. The wrinkles that fanned out from his eyes aged him some, but Josh did not think he was much past forty. He looked very tired. Josh explained in some detail his own relationship with Quanah, leaving out anything that might provide a clue as to the Comanche war chief's whereabouts—not that he had any idea of Quanah's location anyway.

"So you're Quanah's law wrangler?" Sturm said. "That's one for the books. A savage with his own lawyer . . . I'll be damned. Doesn't that make you some kind of an accomplice or something?"

"Believe me, I've thought long and hard about this. Maybe I'm just rationalizing, but I just see myself as a lawyer negotiating the best deal for my client before he turns himself in. If I knew Quanah planned a specific attack, I'd have an obligation to inform the law or the army. But I've never had that kind of information. He has ways of finding me when he wants, but I have no way of knowing where he's at, and, in light of the murder of my contact, I don't know how to get in touch with him right now. He'll find me when he's ready, though. Even then I'll probably just talk to the woman I told you about, She Who Speaks."

"Jael Chernik. I recall something about a Dr. Chernik and his family who got separated from a wagon train some years back and were never heard from again."

"Yes. And the daughter ended up with Quanah's band and made herself pretty much indispensable. She has an unbelievable gift for languages, and she's damned shrewd. She understands the politics of things, and Quanah's smart enough to listen to her."

"I'd like to meet her. But it sounds like she might put me out of business. Let's not tell Mackenzie Quanah's got his own interpreter. I need the money. I'm sure as hell not making it with my doctoring skills." He waved his hand in the direction of his bed-bound patients. "Two starving Comanche. All we can do is feed them for a while and turn them back out on the reservation to go hungry again. The old ones are supposed to go off someplace and die when there's not enough food for everybody."

"I thought the government was providing food allotments."

"When does the government ever do what it promises? The President and even a fair number of Congressmen have good intentions, but the bureaucrats run it all. The government's own agents are very adept at siphoning off the cattle and grains and selling everything on the markets. The Indians don't see half of it."

"This takes me to what I want to talk about. Quanah will use his influence with the other chiefs to bring in his Comanche if three demands are met."

Sturm gave a cynical smile. "I suppose we surrender the state of Texas to the Comanche and kick out all of the whites and Mexicans."

Josh ignored the remark. "No punishment for the Comanche warriors or their chiefs. Land to be owned by, and under total control of, the tribe. And cattle to stock the grazing lands. Quanah wants the tribe to become self-sufficient so his people aren't forced to depend upon the whim of those bureaucrats who are starving your patients."

Sturm raked his fingers through his beard and rubbed his chin thoughtfully. "He's right, of course, but the land will still be reservation property subject to political manipulation in the years ahead. His new warriors will be lawyers."

"I suspect Quanah has healthy political instincts of his own, and I hope to set up an office near the reservation and convince Jael Chernek to manage it as a clerk until she can pass the territorial bar. I haven't told her what I have in mind, but it would be an opportunity for her to help the Comanche as well as herself."

"You seem quite enamored of this woman."

"Not in a romantic way. I just see her as a formidable woman with skills that I would like to harvest for my law firm." Josh detected a note of skepticism in the physician's eyes.

"Well, Josh, I have reason to believe I'm going to be one of the emissaries when the final peace overtures are made . . . and I believe that will be within a year's time . . . so I will certainly get word to the right places. Frankly, though, you're not negotiating with great leverage. The Comanche are on their last legs. They are going to die or surrender. It's just a matter of time. It's a wretched situation. The march of civilization . . . if that's what one would call it . . . stomps those who happen to be in the way. This will be a sorry chapter in our country's history when the books are written about these times."

"I just ask that you do what you can. I don't see Quanah surrendering anytime soon, and there are chiefs in his band with less foresight, who must be convinced of the wisdom of making peace. Unfortunately, many needless deaths will take place on both sides in the meantime."

"Dr. Sturm. I'm sorry to interrupt, but I think you need to take a look at Private Henkel." It was the young nurse calling from the soldier's bedside. The look of alarm on her face did not portend good news.

Sturm got up from his chair and walked deliberately to the far end of the room. He bent over the bed, and Josh saw him take the soldier's wrist in his hand. After a few moments, he announced, "He's gone."

Sturm pulled the blanket over the dead soldier's face and addressed the nurse matter-of-factly. "Get word to the post surgeon. They'll send someone out to pick him up."

The nurse seemed to accept the announcement stoically and hurried away. Josh supposed she had repeated the scene many times before. Sturm returned to his desk and sat down.

"Typhoid," Sturm said. "Most of our military patients are sent here to die. Less disturbing to infirmary patients, I guess. Occasionally, a patient walks out of here, but not often. I put in a claim with the commandant and eventually get paid half of it. I guess a young man could do worse than have Elizabeth's angelic face hovering over him at the time of his departure. She's a kind, caring young woman. Why in the hell she'd want to spend her days doing this baffles me. She'd make more money in the post laundry."

"Some people seem to be born caregivers, and they can't help themselves." He thought of his beloved Cassie and was overtaken by a sudden melancholy. Cassie and Josh and Michael. And then there was one. But there was hope there might be two again. That would please Cassie if she was out there somewhere.

Sturm suddenly dismissed him. "Contact me again in September if you haven't heard from me before. We'll talk specifics."

17

JESSICA WAS NIBBLING on his ear when Josh woke up. Her naked body was snuggled spoon-like against his back, making him wonder why he chose all of those lonely nights on the trail. Maybe his absence made their reunions more treasured.

He rolled over and kissed her softly on her waiting lips. "What time is it?"

"Past nine o'clock," she said. "You're going to get voted out of your own firm if you don't start showing up for work on time."

"I work twenty-four hours a day when I'm not in Santa Fe. I don't owe the firm any time."

She slipped away from him and scooted to the edge of the bed. She sat on the bed a few minutes, and he wondered if she was intentionally provoking him by affording him the view of her slender back and the little crevice of her ass. Probably. And it was working. She leaped up from the bed and began gathering up her clothes, which were strewn about the room.

"I have to get ready for work. The ballet troupe should arrive today."

"Ballet troupe?"

"You've been back a week. The Bella Union Theatre Ballet. From San Francisco. There are signs posted all over town. You've been with me the last five nights. I haven't talked about anything else. You don't listen to a word I say. And by the way, this is making me look like a whore."

"What is?"

"I'm in your room every night. And I don't leave until after sunrise. Everybody knows. Shit, the people in the next room probably hear us."

"You. Not me."

She shot him an annoyed glare, as she pulled on her dress.

"I've offered to come to your room."

"I don't want you in my room. It seems too much like you're moving in. Besides, you tend to be on the slovenly side when it comes to housekeeping."

"You seem to make yourself comfortable when you're here." They had spent a few nights in her room, and Josh found it so immaculate and organized he was ill at ease there. Fortunately, Jessica preferred his room for their lovemaking trysts.

She ignored him. "I won't see you tonight. I'll be working with the Bella group setting up the stage for their performance. By the way, my new piano arrived yesterday with the wagons that came in. The troupe has their own violins and a magnificent pianist. But there weren't any decent pianos in Santa Fe . . . until now."

"How much did the piano cost the shareholders?"

"You don't want to know."

She was sufficiently clothed now for the escape to her own room.

"When will I see you?"

"Unless you want to help out as a stage hand, I'll see you tomorrow night for opening night. The shareholders will be introduced before the performance. And you will be one of the hosts here at the Exchange following the performance. Remember?"

"Sorry. I forgot." He rolled his eyes. "I wouldn't miss it."

She gave him the look again before she slipped out the door. "No, I don't think you would dare."

18

DANNA WAS AT her desk reading *The New Mexican* when Josh tapped on the door and entered the office. He sat down while she continued to read. After a few moments Danna folded the paper and passed it across the desk. "Take it with you," she said. "Your sister has claimed the entire front page."

Josh picked up the newspaper and perused the front page. He saw three Tabitha Rivers bylines on separate stories. Impressive. God, he hoped she didn't get herself killed—or worse —traipsing around Comanche country with the U.S. Army.

"Her dispatches came all in one sweep so *The New Mexican* says there will be a week's worth of stories. They're calling it the Red River War. Tabby promised me she'd name it that."

"She's named a war? My little sister?"

"It appears so. Besides her daring, she's a brilliant writer. Her story about a family of slaughtered settlers forced me to relive a part of my own life."

"Maybe she was reliving part of her own."

"Could be. You've got something on your mind?"

"Several things. You've been so tied up with legal business, we haven't had a chance to talk since I got back."

"Business is booming. We're handling three major land grant disputes right now, and Lucien Maxwell has hired the firm to represent the First National Bank of Santa Fe. This is an enormous opportunity for the firm. Until the Second National organized two years ago, it was the only bank within four hundred miles. And now I've received discreet inquiries from one of the Spiegelberg brothers about whether we'd be interested in doing some work for Second National."

Josh had met several of the brothers but was never clear on which brother bore which first name. The Spiegelbergs were German Jews. There were five brothers, who had opened the bank in a corner of their huge mercantile store. Josh had done some real estate work for Willi Spiegelberg and had met Levi in the Spiegelberg Brothers store, the largest business on the Plaza. He was not acquainted with Emanuel, Lehman or Jacob. The banking business was dwarfed by Maxwell's First National, but Josh had no doubt about the Second National Bank's ultimate success. "Can we represent both banks? Are there conflict of interest problems?"

"They're competitors, but they're not adversaries in the legal sense. It is unlikely that either would have reason to sue the other. If so, we'd have to disqualify ourselves from representing either. Our work would be mostly real estate related. Mortgages, title searches, foreclosures and that sort of thing. What I've been learning about corporate structuring would be useful. I would want to get Maxwell's approval before we took on the Spiegelbergs. The Second National knew of that relationship before the contact, so there should be no problem on that end."

"You seem to have it figured out."

"Would you talk to Lucien Maxwell? I know he's a friend of your father's. And he should talk with the firm's senior partner. I think you said a piece of the Slash R came from the Maxwell grant."

"It did. If Lucien's in town, I'll speak with him today."

"He is. Linda made an appointment for you at the bank at two o'clock."

A year ago, her presumptiveness would have annoyed him considerably, but now it earned only a passive thought. He changed the subject. "What about Marty? How is he working out?"

"Magnificently. He's very versatile, totally comfortable in the courtroom but more than willing to take on anything I throw at him from the office practice. To establish a bit of separation, I plan to have him focus on the Second National legal matters while I retain responsibility for the First National account. He works like a man obsessed. He's often here when I leave at night."

That was saying something, because Danna was no slacker when it came to logging in office hours. "He seems to be keeping my desk clear. It's nice to get back and not find a pile of work waiting."

"He's a fit for us. But within a year we'll need another lawyer."

He was going to have to slow this woman down. "Let's talk about it then."

"Now what did you really want to talk about?"

"I've got two concerns, and they both involve Comanche."

"One is Michael, I assume."

"Yes. It's getting close to a month and no word from Pierce.

It makes me nervous."

"He said it could be a month, didn't he? And who knows in that godforsaken country what kinds of delays they could have run into? I don't think you can assume that the delay means anything."

"Well, on my way back from Fort Sill I lined up the ransom . . . I hope. I stopped at the Slash R and talked to Pop. It didn't take a second to sign him on. I just hope he doesn't have to deal with disappointment. He signed a letter of guaranty to the First National backing any loans I might take out for ransom money. That's another reason I'm glad to speak with Lucien."

"I can understand that."

"On the way to Pop's I stopped to see Erin and Cal."

"And how are they? Is Cal still domesticated?"

"Very much so. He dotes on Willow, who is a beautiful child. Dark eyes and lightly-bronzed skin hinting of her Comanche ancestry. No trace of Erin's red hair. But that's not all."

"Yes?"

"There's going to be a wedding."

"Cal and Erin?"

"Yes. The clan will travel to Santa Fe in July for the nuptials. There's a Presbyterian Church that started up here awhile back, and Cal said they're desperate enough they'll marry anybody. New Mexico isn't exactly fertile ground for Protestants. Erin wants to have Willow baptized the same day."

He noticed Danna's smile seemed forced. He always suspected that Cal and Danna had shared a romantic interlude of some kind—probably an intimate one, knowing his brother, and Danna's subdued reaction confirmed it. He hated giving her the rest of the news. "There's something else. Erin's pregnant."

"Pregnant? How did that happen?" Danna looked incredulous. "I mean, I know how it happened. I just have trouble seeing Cal suddenly becoming such a family man."

"You and me both. But he's getting there damned fast."

"Well, I'm glad for both of them."

She seemed sincere, or at least had quickly come to terms with the news. It was time to move on to something else. "I told you I thought we'd made some progress on Quanah's behalf. I think Dr. Sturm will be a valuable ally. He has no decision-making power, but important people in the chain of authority evidently listen to him. For the first time I feel I've made some headway. It all comes down to amnesty, land and cattle. I'd like to communicate with Quanah, but I don't know how to reach him right now."

"You said he would find you when he was ready."

"But I'm ready now. He's paid us well, and I'm anxious to let him know I've opened a door."

"I think he's paying us as much for what he expects us to do after the peace as before."

"You're probably right. I'll give him a month, and then, if I haven't received any word, I'll head for the southern Staked Plains and he'll find me."

"Or somebody you don't want to find you will. Be patient. You have enough trouble coming your way without looking for it."

19

Josh surmised that the Bella Union Theatre Ballet performance was superb, if audience reaction were the measure. Cynically, he doubted if the attendees knew any more about the art form than he did. This was his first exposure to stage performance of ballet, and he decided he would not suffer greatly if this turned out to be his last. He did enjoy the music. To his untrained ear, the young pianist and single violinist performed admirably, and the pianist was pleasing to the eye. She had flaxen hair—almost an oddity in Santa Fe—and was petite with fine features. He guessed she would be in her early twenties. The violinist was a lean, darker man, who would blend with the local populace easily, Josh thought. From the interplay with their eyes, Josh would bet they were sleeping together.

The dance group consisted of five performers: four women and one man. They were very athletic, and it was fascinating to watch them glide and twirl on the stage. Two of the women were slender just short of bony, and an auburn-haired ballerina sported curves where a woman should. The fourth was a bit on the pudgy side but appeared to be quite muscular.

The music and dancing stopped, and Jessica stepped onto the stage. She had a presence and bearing that made her a natural there, and Josh looked forward to seeing her perform in a play called "Checkmate" that would be performed in August. She was a remarkable and vivacious woman, and tonight, he thought, she looked simply stunning in a burgundy dress that somehow contrasted perfectly with her milk-white skin, which she protected religiously from the scorching Santa Fe sun.

"There will be a fifteen-minute intermission," she announced. "There will be free tea and coffee with a nice assortment of cookies in the lobby." She paused. "There is also a nice selection of wines and other spirits for those who are so inclined. Unfortunately, we must assess a charge for those. We look forward to your return to enjoy the remainder of the evening's performance."

Josh was certain that the captive husbands and other escorts would help fill theatre coffers at the spirits table. He appreciated that Jessica was very astute when it came to the business side of the theatre. He and most of the ten or so shareholders had not expected huge returns on their investments, but they had certainly hoped they would not be hit up for additional contributions to capital. It appeared that Jessica had management skills that gave some assurance the theatre would at least, after payment of Jessica's salary and revenue shares, be self-sustaining. The theatre had been packed to its ninety-seat capacity, and that meant the patrons had to squeeze into the lobby. Josh inched his way through the crowd, picked up a cup of coffee, and wedged himself into a corner of the room. As he surveyed the theatre-goers, he caught sight of Marty and Danna across the room with wine glasses in their hands. If he knew Danna, the two were just business colleagues being seen at the right places. Danna's eyes met his, and she gave a quick wave, which he returned. Then he realized the beautiful Constanza Hildalgo was only a half dozen feet from him, accompanied by her betrothed, Judge Andrew Robinson.

Constanza and Josh had been lovers for more than a year before the relationship shattered, more because of his unwillingness to marry than anything. She was a passionate and energetic lover with a fiery temper to match. Her father, Miguel, did not approve of the romance, and most of their assignations occurred when Miguel was not in town. He knew Connie would have eloped with him, but he realized also that their romance, for better or worse, was not an enduring one. It saddened him some, though, to see her with the Territorial District Court Judge, who was more than twenty years her senior. It was to be a marriage arranged by her father to merge the judge's influence and power with the Hidalgo fortune. Connie would make the best of it, but Robinson, the pompous ass, had better not count on her fidelity.

Josh started when a hand tapped his shoulder. He turned to see Linda de la Cruz, a worried look on her face. "Linda, what is it?"

"I was working late at the office, and Mr. Pierce knocked on the door. I let him in. He seemed very upset and said he needed to see you immediately. He said there is a problem."

"Where is he?"

"He's waiting in the office. I can send him away if you wish, but I thought you would want to know."

"You were right. Would you go back and tell him I'll be there shortly? I need a few minutes to make my excuses."

Josh cast his eyes about the room, looking for Jessica. He

finally spotted her, surrounded by admirers making their way back into the theatre. Perhaps she wouldn't miss him. Like hell she wouldn't. He headed for the door anyway.

20

TABITHA FOUND HERSELF traveling as the sole woman with over five hundred soldiers now. Lieutenant Sean Kelly's small company had merged with the Sixth Cavalry and Fifth Infantry from Fort Dodge, Kansas, under the command of Colonel Nelson A. Miles. The colonel and his troops carried reputations as formidable Indian fighters, and Tabitha took Miles' involvement as an indication that something huge was brewing in what she continued to call the Red River War.

There were at least four other correspondents with the troops now, but she welcomed the competition. Just let them try to out-write or out-think her. She had the nose for a story and was confident in her skill to tell it in an interesting way, slicing unnecessary words like a butcher with a meat cleaver. She didn't get to see many of her words in print, but her editor at *The New Mexican*, in the letters that reached her, kept urging her to produce more stories and indicated the publisher had now contracted with a syndicate that was publishing her work in the East. He did not say anything about a raise. She would deal with that when she returned to Santa Fe.

She and Lieutenant Kelly had become fast friends. She was genuinely fond of Sean, but she sensed his feelings were much more intense. He thought he was in love with her, she admitted. She carried a bit of guilt about that because she did not want to hurt him. She did not view him as a potential suitor or lover—well, not yet, anyway. He was also a source of information and background for her stories, but he surrendered no military secrets —if there were any. All the soldiers talked among themselves about where the army was headed and what the strategy was. All one had to do was listen and then attempt to filter fact from fiction. Regardless, there were hundreds of stories to be told out here on the Texas plains with these men of such disparate backgrounds and histories.

Sean Kelly rode up beside her and tipped his hat in greeting. The heat was suffocating this June afternoon, and, though the horses mostly walked because of the snail's pace of the supply wagons, the troops still moved in a giant cloud of dust.

"We're about forty miles south of the Red River," the lieutenant said. "Almost back to where we turned north several weeks ago."

"It doesn't make much sense to go all that way north to meet up with Colonel Miles's troops and then come back again. Wouldn't it have made more sense to wait at the river and meet up there?"

"Theirs is not to reason why; theirs but to do and die. That's a soldier's lot."

"Into the valley of death rode the six hundred. Tennyson. Morbid, considering where we're at right now."

Sean grinned sheepishly. He did have an irresistible smile, damn him. And she liked that he shared her love of books and literature.

"I have a question," Tabitha said. "I thought we were going to meet up with the famous Brevet General Mackenzie at Adobe Walls. I wanted an interview."

"Well, I arranged an interview for you with Colonel Miles."

"Yes, I'll give you credit for that. He made a good interview. I sent the story out with the courier yesterday. But I want Bad Hand himself."

"Well, the talk of meeting him at Adobe Walls was rumor. I have it on good authority that Mackenzie is far south at Fort Concho . . . or will be soon. Eventually, we'll meet up with his Fourth Cavalry. Black Jack Davidson's Tenth Cavalry will be riding out from Fort Sill, and Major Bill Price will march out from Fort Bascomb, New Mexico with the Eighth Cavalry, which my company's a part of. There will be more than three thousand soldiers in the field."

"I thought there are only about a thousand Comanche remaining off the reservation, and perhaps only a third of those are warriors."

"Nobody really knows, but somebody up the line decided overwhelming force would be the order of the day. Also, there are a significant number of Comanche that go back and forth to and from the reservation. The Fort Sill commandant says there are a lot of absences right now. And, of course, there are sizable bands of Kiowa aligned with Quanah."

Tabitha made mental notes while they spoke, hoping she could remember everything till she got to pen and paper. She sensed that the lieutenant was providing her with foundation information for stories that would carry banner headlines and that by the time they appeared in print would not compromise the army's strategy.

They were interrupted when a rider approached their place in the column, urging his mount at breakneck speed. "Lieutenant, Lieutenant, orders from Colonel Miles."

Kelly rode out to meet him, and Tabitha tagged along. The young private reined in his horse in front of them. "Lieutenant, sir, the colonel has ordered that you move out with Company Two and head back to Adobe Walls."

"Return to Adobe Walls?"

"Yes, sir. He just received word from a buffalo hunter that the occupants are under attack by Comanches . . . lots of them. You're to assist the hunters there and then catch up with our troops after you've secured the settlement."

"Tell the colonel we're on our way."

"Yes, sir." The private saluted, wheeled his horse and disappeared quickly into the haze of dust.

Lieutenant Kelly turned to Tabitha. "You'll probably want to stay with the main column."

"Like hell," she snapped. "I smell a story. And it will be an exclusive. None of those tenderfeet will be up to covering this." The other correspondents represented Eastern newspapers and were not accustomed to the rugged riding called for on the plains. The journey was just starting, and they were wearing down fast, she had noticed in sizing up her competition. They could barely drag themselves to their whiskey bottles after a hard day in the saddle. Of course, she could outride anyone in this man's army, if you didn't count White Wolf. He was melded to his big Appaloosa stallion and one of the few riders she'd ever seen that she envied.

Kelly signaled his sergeants and the two scouts to join him.

After he explained their mission, White Wolf and Rattlesnake raced their horses away from the slow-moving main column, Rattlesnake heading northeasterly and White Wolf riding toward the northwest. The sergeants pulled the soldiers of Company Two from the main column, and in a matter of minutes they were retracing their trail back to Adobe Walls.

21

Lieutenant Kelly had halted his troops at dusk to rest both horses and troops. There was a spring nearby to replenish water supplies and a small waterhole fed by the spring to provide water for the horses. Rattlesnake had returned and warned that there were few water sources in the area and that the Comanche would know about this one, also. And there were many Comanche, perhaps as many as three hundred within a half day's ride. He speculated that any attack on Adobe Walls was probably over because the war parties were not on the move in any direction. He thought this meant serious councils were in session.

The lieutenant doubled the sentries for the night and ordered the sergeants to have the troops ready to ride before dawn. He expected to reach Adobe Walls by late afternoon. Tabitha crawled into her bedroll, but sleep would not come, and she was awake when White Wolf rode into camp with another rider. The other man appeared to have his hands tied behind his back, and she saw White Wolf dismount and walk over to the stranger and yank him harshly from the horse and toss him on the ground. She pushed her blankets back and got up and joined

White Wolf at the same moment Lieutenant Kelly and Rattlesnake arrived.

"I have spoken with this man," White Wolf said. "I was going to kill him, but I thought better of it. He seems quite talkative with only a small amount of persuasion."

Tabitha could see that Sean Kelly was as taken aback as she at the scout's perfect English delivered with only the slightest tinge of a Southern accent. She thought there might be a story there.

White Wolf pulled the Comanche to his feet. He was nearly naked, wearing only a breechclout to cover his loins and a wide deerskin band that covered much of his forehead. White Wolf spoke with the captive, apparently using a combination of Comanche and sign language.

"My Comanche vocabulary is very limited, but I can tell you what I learned earlier. This man was headed back to the reservation when I caught him alone. I don't think he's much of a warrior . . . probably joined the war party to partake in the looting. There are many, many Comanche between here and Adobe Walls, although they are starting to split off now. This man says the Comanche and Kiowa did not overtake Adobe Walls and suffered many losses in spite of Isa-tai's promise they would be immune to the white men's bullets. Isa-tai is a chief or shaman with a large following, but I gather he lost some influence after the disaster at Adobe Walls. Lieutenant, do you have some questions of this man?"

"Yes. Ask him if Quanah was there."

White Wolf and the Comanche began speaking and signing at what seemed a frantic pace. The Comanche was turning belligerent until his interrogator pulled a knife from its sheath and spoke sharply, waving the blade over the hapless Indian's groin. The prisoner spoke at some length, after which White Wolf turned to Kelly and said, "I told him I would cut off his penis and stuff it in his mouth before I killed him. I made it clear that I was serious."

Kelly responded, "But you wouldn't have?"

The look in White Wolf's eyes answered the Lieutenant's question. "This man says Quanah was there, and he may have been wounded . . . probably not seriously."

"But our troops are all converging toward the central Staked Plains. He's not even close to where they're headed. We need to get word to Colonel Miles."

"They will have disappeared like ghosts by the time the colonel moves a contingent of that size back north. They will not move further north, so they will retreat back to the country they know. And their women and children are in that land . . . the bait, in a sense. The Comanche will not desert their families. Your Colonel Mackenzie's strategy is sound."

"Our orders were to go to Adobe Walls, so we will continue on our march there tomorrow morning."

"Lieutenant, you are in command, and I will follow your instructions, but may I offer a suggestion or two?"

"Certainly."

Tabitha watched and listened with curiosity. White Wolf had the strange presence of authority. It reminded her that the casual judgment of men and women was very fallible. Initial impressions were untrustworthy. A person's attire told you nothing about the mind or the character or skills that lay within the camouflage.

"I suspect the Comanche and Kiowa bands will be splitting

up and riding back to their own villages. But they are angry and pity anyone in their paths. And, Lieutenant, we are in the path of at least some of them. Several bands will in all likelihood ride toward these springs for the same reason we stopped here. We're going to encounter them if we continue on to Adobe Walls, and they will sweep in and attack the column again and again as we move north. If there are the numbers I fear, there may not be one of us remaining to tell our story. It is open country, and there is no place to set up a defense."

"Then we'll charge head on. They can't match our weaponry."

"And they will get out of the way, and you will fire and slash at nothing, while you are attacked from the rear. They learned there is no cloak of invincibility at Adobe Walls. They will not make that mistake again."

"You speak like someone who has had military experience."

"Major. First Cherokee Brigade, Confederate Army."

"I see. I don't know what the hell you're doing here . . . pardon me, Miss Rivers . . . but it doesn't matter, I guess. What do you suggest?"

"Stay put. You've got water to wait out a siege, although that's unlikely since they'll want to move on quickly. More important, you have time to fortify a position. The ground is a little higher here, and you've got a rocky terrain. I'd circle the springs with nine or ten stone fortifications that would provide cover for four or five men each. There are some dead cottonwoods that could be drug over to provide more cover. Stake the horses outside the ring so they aren't in the direct line of fire, but put extra men near the mounts because the Comanche would like to make off with the animals."

"You make sense. I'll take your advice." He turned back

toward the camp and yelled, "Sergeant Riley, on the double."

Tabitha gained new respect for Sean Kelly at that moment. It took an exceptional young officer to heed the counsel of another—especially a civilian scout—in devising critical military strategy at a moment of crisis. Soldiers would not die needlessly because of Lieutenant Kelly's ego.

White Wolf spoke again. "With the Lieutenant's permission, Rattlesnake and I will head out and scout out the enemy's location and numbers. I hope we can report back that your preparations have been unnecessary and that we can proceed to Adobe Walls as ordered."

"Permission granted."

Tabitha didn't think the Lieutenant had even noticed that White Wolf wrestled the Comanche prisoner back on the horse and led the animal out of the camp as he and Rattlesnake rode out. She hoped White Wolf would turn the Indian loose and send him on his way to the reservation. She knew, also, she would never ask.

22

THE SOLDIERS WORKED feverishly, rolling and pushing stones into small barricades rising no more than three feet from the rock-littered earth. Tabitha helped with the staking of the horses, which at the Lieutenant's order were kept saddled. Whether this was for possible escape or readiness for some suicidal charge, she had no idea.

The reality of the situation suddenly struck her. She was no longer a writer observing and reporting a story. She was a part of the story, and she might never live to write it. She remembered her dueling verses with Sean yesterday afternoon and recalled more lines from Tennyson's "The Charge of the Light Brigade": *Into the jaws of death, into the mouth of hell rode the six hundred.* Was this his mouth of hell? She had seen firsthand Comanche handiwork. She could not imagine a hell worse than what had been rendered at those scenes of savagery. She had known fear in her life, but on other occasions it had been suddenly thrust upon her, and she had only to react. The angst of waiting for the unknown was far worse.

Soldiers were beginning to move into the placements with

their rifles and other weaponry as Tabitha left the remuda. Lieutenant Kelly approached her, his face glum. "I am sending a courier to inform Colonel Miles of our situation. I can spare two more men. I would like you to ride with them. It's a much safer option, and I know you and Smokey can outride them."

"No," she said flatly, thinking as the word came out that she was a fool.

"I can order you."

"Yes, but you can't make me obey. I'm not leaving."

Lieutenant Kelly shrugged and walked away.

Tabitha found her Winchester and bag of ammunition, snatched up her canteen, and slipped behind a barricade with Sergeant Riley and two young privates. "Can you use another gun here?" she asked. The portly, gray-haired Riley looked at her questioningly and then smiled. "Yes, ma'am. Make yourself at home. Can you shoot as well as you ride?"

"Better."

"Then you're more than welcome here."

More than an hour of eerie silence dragged by. Other than the occasional whinny of a horse, not a sound broke the night air. The tension seemed contagious, each man's anxiety and nervousness feeding off of his comrades. A sliver of sunlight pressed above the western horizon, and at that moment, the sound of hoof beats alerted the encampment. One rider, Tabitha decided, racing toward the soldiers. As the horse neared, she could tell it was Rattlesnake from his low set in the saddle.

The Tonkawa reined in his horse and slipped onto the ground in what seemed a single motion. The lieutenant paced deliberately out to meet him. They were beyond easy earshot, but their hands were animated, and Rattlesnake was obviously excited. Soon the grim-faced lieutenant returned to his troops, while the Tonkawa led the exhausted horse away.

"They'll be here in an hour or less," Kelly announced. "Rattlesnake says there could be as many as a hundred Comanche. Just remember they probably don't have as many rifles as we do, and very few will have the marksmanship skills with the guns. Don't fire until you hear the order. Those who carry Sharps will fire on the first command. You have a longer range. Other rifles will commence firing on the second order. Don't waste your ammunition. Rattlesnake says they will try to run us over and swarm in for hand to hand. If we can stop that, we can wear them down. At some point we can make their losses unacceptable. They've already been in one battle. These warriors are not fresh."

The Comanche still outnumbered them two to one, Tabitha thought. And the fact they had fewer rifles mattered only a little. Comanche arrows would be true, and in hand to hand combat, the war clubs and axes would be unlike anything these young soldiers had ever encountered. Sean, with the exception of a few sergeants and corporals, was not commanding battle-hardened soldiers.

A half hour later, White Wolf appeared like an apparition out of the hazy dawn and led his speckled Appaloosa into the middle of the fortifications. "They are here," he said. "You cannot see them, but they have arrived."

As if on cue, lines of Comanche appeared silently on the north and eastern horizons. To Tabitha's eye, the lines were endless, and it seemed there were thousands, but she knew her imagination was just taking hold. She felt at once a lump of terror in her throat and regret she had not learned the growing art of photography that would have allowed her to capture this frightening and magnificent scene. If she somehow lived through this day, she vowed to add that skill to her journalistic repertoire.

She heard White Wolf discussing the battle plan with Sean, who seemed amazingly calm and collected for his first time under enemy attack. The lieutenant then ordered that half the soldiers at each battle station move with the thrust of the enemy to barricades to assist with the points of direct attack until the troops were fully encircled, as would probably eventually be the case. At that point the designated swing men were to resume their original stations.

Suddenly, the Comanche moved forward in waves, their horses becoming a thundering herd that nearly drowned out the whoops and battle cries of the skilled riders. Tabitha felt like she was the only target of the onslaught and that the attackers were aimed at her position. Momentarily, three more soldiers squeezed behind the barricade, barely leaving room to maneuver the rifles. She could see the faces of some of the Comanche now, fearsome and almost grotesque behind the masks of war paint.

"Fire!" came the lieutenant's order from somewhere behind her. The rifles roared almost in unison, and a half dozen Comanche tumbled from their horses. Several horses went down with their riders. But the Indians swept forward. Tabitha felt they were almost upon her and was impatient to fire her own rifle. What was Sean waiting for?

"Fire at will!"

Tabitha squeezed the trigger. Her first shot missed, but the second struck an attacker's neck and she could see instant eruption of blood before he slumped off the horse. Her first kill, and it left her unfazed. Her angst evaporated, and now her concentration focused on the next target, and the next.

The Comanche were taking heavy casualties, and dead and wounded warriors and horses littered the ground. Suddenly, the wave split and the riders broke off to right and left, thinning their ranks, and, as predicted, encircling the defenders. The attackers moved out of gunfire range, and some, who were evidently chiefs of some kind, rode back and forth, speaking with each other and then returning to others, waving their arms and signaling something. During the lull in the fighting, two of the soldiers left the barricade and returned to their own stations. Only then did she notice the unmoving soldier crumpled on the ground beside her. The side of his face had been smashed by a bullet and was painted scarlet with blood. He had also taken an arrow in the throat. He had died soundlessly in the heat of battle no more than two feet from her placement, and she had not even known.

Sergeant Riley lumbered to his feet, grabbed the private's feet and dragged him to the center of the camp, where other dead and wounded lay. By Tabitha's count, there were at least six dead and that many more wounded. There was no surgeon with the company, and several untrained troopers had been assigned to tend the injured. Her first instinct was to move to assist with the wounded, but a fresh assault by the Comanche pulled her back to her firing position. She sensed someone moving in beside her and filling the void left by the dead soldier. Looking out of the corner of her eye, she saw it was White Wolf. Neither spoke as they waited for the Comanche to near and then began to fire their rifles.

Comanche continued to fall but so did troopers. The Comanche would charge toward the embattled company and then abruptly wheel away. Tabitha noted that with each attack the warriors inched closer until now they were as near as twenty-five feet distant. Then some of the presumed dead or wounded Comanche began to rise from the ground and race forward with lances or war clubs upraised. Several had invaded the circle of defense now and were engaged in the dreaded hand to hand. While she was reloading, a near-naked warrior leaped over the stone fortification and arced his axe down toward her skull. As she raised her gun to ward off the blow, a knife blade sunk under the Comanche's ribcage, and he fell backward with White Wolf on top of him. White Wolf yanked back the knife and sliced the blade across the warrior's throat for good measure and, just as quickly, returned to his firing position.

The Comanche seemed to be pulling back some when Tabitha caught sight of warriors dragging two hapless young troopers by their hair and arms away from the camp. She fired repeatedly at two of the warriors who had captured one soldier and took them down, allowing him to crawl away under cover of fire. The other soldier was being carried away now by a half dozen warriors to others with awaiting horses. Seemingly out of nowhere, Lieutenant Kelly erupted and gave chase with his Army Colt blazing. Several soldiers fell in behind him, and the encampment's fire turned on the captors, who dropped the soldier and leaped on their horses. But in a final taunt, a tall muscular warrior heaved his lance as the enraged lieutenant closed in, and it drove true, entering Sean Kelly's chest and the point burrowing out between his shoulder blades.

The Comanche were withdrawing, at least temporarily, and soldiers instantly raced to the battlefield and retrieved their wounded commanding officer. White Wolf joined them as they moved the lieutenant into the defense circle. The scout broke off the long shaft of the lance and cut off the point that erupted through the back, making it easier to maneuver the wounded officer's body. Tabitha moved to his side and could see his chest rising and falling in labored breaths. It was a mortal wound, and she could only offer comfort during his final moments. She scooted next to him and lifted his head so it rested on her lap. His eyes opened and he blinked,

"Tabby, is that you?"

She caressed his cheek softly. "It is, Sean. Just rest now."

"You're beautiful. The most beautiful woman I've ever known."

"Thank you, Sean," she said, knowing that with her dust- and blood-caked face, she was far from his vision of her. "And you are the most handsome man I've ever known."

He smiled and closed his eyes, and his breaths became shallow before they faded away to nothing. She held him for some minutes after he was gone, making no attempt to hide the rivulets of tears that rolled down her cheeks. She released him only when Sergeant Riley's gravelly voice warned, "The Comanche are coming. Back to your positions."

"Sergeant, I'd tell your men not to fire," White Wolf interjected. "They're returning for their dead and wounded. If we let them do this in peace, I think they'll call it quits and move on."

"I guess we got nothing to lose." He called to the troops, "Hold your fire."

Riley even ordered three dead Comanche within the circle carried out to their tribesmen and placed on the ground. The Indians watched with suspicious eyes until the soldiers retreated.

When all of the dead had been slung over horses and the wounded mounted or placed on travois to be dragged away behind horses, the Comanche moved out silently. And as White Wolf had speculated, the battle was over.

Sergeant Riley, as the senior sergeant, took command. There were now twelve dead to be buried and that many more wounded who required medical assistance. He decided that the remnants of Company B should move south and rejoin the Miles column. Tabitha insisted she must go on to Adobe Walls. She tried to convince the Sergeant that if several troopers joined her, they would be able to evaluate the situation there and report back to Miles, thus still completing the original mission. After heated argument, the Sergeant gave in and ordered two troopers and White Wolf to accompany Tabitha to Adobe Walls and to join the main column "damn fast."

23

IT WAS PITCH black outside when Josh arrived at the Rivers and Sinclair offices. There was only a sliver of moon in the sky, and a rare cloud cover obscured most of the stars. There was a light in the waiting room as well as his personal office, so Linda, always a step ahead, must have lighted the new kerosene lamps before she came to fetch him at the ballet performance. Jess would be pissed when she learned of his early departure, and she would be suspicious of any excuse, but when he explained, she would grant him absolution, he was confident. Besides, the performance was a splendid success, and she would be consumed the next four days with the encore presentations.

When he entered his office, Clayborne Pierce stood and extended his hand. Josh accepted warily. The man had obviously not shaved for days, and he looked haggard and wasted. His clothes were wrinkled and dirty. This was not the dandy Josh had met more than a month before in Santa Fe.

"You said it was urgent that you see me."

"It's about the search for your son." He pulled a small leather bag from his coat pocket and handed it to Josh. "I'm refunding your payment. I can't help you."

"I think I'm due an explanation. Come on into my office."

Josh led the way to his private office and sat down in the chair at his desk, gesturing with his hand that Pierce should take the chair across from him. "Now tell me what this is all about."

"Offers for ransom are clearly not being considered for your son, Michael."

"You located him?"

"In a manner of speaking."

"What does that mean?"

"I don't know where he's living at this particular moment, but I know who he's with."

"Get to the point, Pierce. Who is he supposedly with?"

"Quanah's band of Kwahadi."

Josh was stunned at the statement. "That can't be."

"Screeching Owl and I rode out to Palo Duro Canyon country, and I camped there while my Tonk colleague went out to search out his Comanche friend. Before he left, he told me that his contact was Kwahadi and that the man had assured him Michael was being raised in Quanah's band. He said there was a scar on the boy's arm. He may or may not have obtained it during his captivity."

"His left arm, just above the elbow. He pulled over a kerosene lantern when he was just starting to walk, and it shattered on the floor. He stumbled and fell on the glass. He had three or four cuts, but the arm wound was particularly nasty. My mother had to do serious stitching."

"Green-tinted brown eyes and rust-brown hair. Sound familiar?"

"My own. My God. It must be Michael." He suddenly felt

deeply betrayed. By Quanah and by She Who Speaks. And he was working for these people. Taking Quanah's gold. They had to know, and they had lied to him by deception and silence, if nothing else. "You knew these things and didn't feel obligated to tell me?"

"If I had told you, it would have accomplished nothing. You would have pressed for more. I didn't know which band had him, because, as I explained, Screeching Owl was instructed not to tell me before I met with our clients. He informed me before he left to make the contact. That was the first I knew of the location."

"So you know where he's at, or who he's with. I don't understand why you're returning your fee."

"I can't help you. The boy cannot be ransomed."

"I don't understand. Why not?"

"I received a message."

"What kind of message?"

"Screeching Owl finally returned to my camp. He had found his Comanche friend, but some other Comanche discovered them both. They were both tortured. One of Owl's eyes was burned out with hot coals, leaving most of the right side of his face a mass of red, swollen pus-oozing wounds. They cut out his tongue as well. He signed that his Comanche contact had been killed. Owl was released to inform me that I would meet an even worse fate if I attempted to contact them about the boy again. Screeching Owl rode out the next morning to go back to his people on the reservation. He was a friend, and I regret the terrible things that happened to him. I think it is time for me to seek out another line of work. The last of the Comanche will be coming in soon anyway. And their captives will be with them. Sorting them out will be a nasty business."

Josh pushed the leather bag of coins back across the table. "You earned this. Our deal was that you would tell me the location if you couldn't accomplish the ransom. And you were to keep the initial payment. You've done that part, and I thank you for it. I'm sorry about your partner. Your information helps me more than you could know."

The two men stood and shook hands. "You're an honorable man, Mr. Rivers. I hope you can recover Michael."

"I will, Mr. Pierce, you can count on it."

24

THE EVENING FOLLOWING his meeting with Clayborne Pierce, Josh did his penance and attended the ballet performance again. This time he did not miss a turn-out or pirouette and remained until the last standing ovation had ended.

Jessica had evidently appreciated his effort to return to her good graces, for she had awakened him with a kiss, after letting herself in with her key at nearly two o'clock in the morning. Thereafter, she had proceeded with a performance worthy itself of a standing ovation, he thought.

Josh sat at a corner table in the Exchange Hotel now, enjoying his morning coffee with a plate of scrambled eggs and a slice of thick sourdough bread covered with an unidentifiable purple jam that he found quite agreeable. His face was hidden behind the pages of *The New Mexican* as he read the recent reports of his little sister from the Red River War. She certainly knew how to turn a phrase and lay out a spellbinding narrative. He felt a sense of family pride as he read her stories and more than a little concern for her safety as he learned of her adventures on the Staked Plains.

Tabby had arrived at Adobe Walls just a few days after a hodgepodge crew of buffalo hunters, skinners, merchants and drovers staved off an attack by a massive force of Comanche and Kiowa warriors. The trading post consisted of a saloon and two stores, and the defenders included twenty-eight men and one woman.

The attackers numbered over two hundred fifty according to Tabby's account, but the buildings were constructed of sod walls that were two feet thick, and the occupants had the merchants' virtual arsenal of ammunition and new Sharps rifles at their disposal. The "big fifties" rifles were manufactured for buffalo hunting and could "nail a big bull at one thousand yards," according to a gambler by the name of Bat Masterson, who was oft quoted in the articles. When the fighting was over, the defenders of Adobe Walls suffered only three deaths, and the Indian losses were at least fifty, according to one count, not including the wounded. Tabby noted, though, that the casualty loss seemed to grow with each telling of the tale.

Tabitha Rivers was the first journalist at the scene, and Josh speculated that her collection of stories about the battle of Adobe Walls would be a huge career boost. She was sure as hell earning it.

"Mr. Rivers?"

Josh looked up from his newspaper and saw a stocky man with thinning gray hair standing at the table. He was a fashionably attired man with an impressive diamond pin fastened to a silk, burgundy-colored cravat.

Josh nodded. "Mr. McKenna."

"May I sit down a moment?"

Josh hesitated and then his curiosity won out. "Yeah, I guess so. Why not?"

Oliver McKenna pulled out a chair across from Josh and sat down. "You must be reading about your sister's exploits. Fascinating stuff. She's a very talented young writer . . . with a barrel of grit, I might add. You must be proud of her."

Josh did not acknowledge the man's remarks. "You obviously didn't sit down to talk about my sister, McKenna. Why don't you just spit it out?"

McKenna shrugged. "Very well. It's come to my attention that you believe that I've retained hired guns to kill you. I want to assure you I have not."

"And why should I believe that?"

"Because I'm telling you the truth. Why would I want you killed? I don't like you, but there are many people I'm not fond of, and I don't arrange for their murders. As you know, Mr. Rivers, I am a wealthy man. I have too much to lose to risk a hangman's noose. I am not a stupid man. All of my enterprises operate within boundaries of the law."

"You weren't above trying to steal your niece's ranch while she was a Comanche captive."

"I thought she was dead. That left me as my brother's only heir. My claim was pursued through the courts, not with hired guns. I had every legal right to do so. I understand we have no love for each other as a result of that case. But your firm won fair and square. I don't have time to harbor a grudge . . . and certainly have no motive to kill because of it."

"Okay, I've listened. Now I need to get to my office." Josh slid his chair back.

"I have more to say, and I suggest you hear me out. I may be able to help you."

Josh scooted his chair back to the table but did not respond.

McKenna continued. "It's true that several of the men who have participated in attacks on you were former employees of mine. They were hired gunslingers . . . and not very good ones it appears, but I had discharged them long before their altercations with you."

"Because they were incompetent?"

"Because they served no purpose in my operations. My enterprises are primarily ranching and mining. There was a time when I required men who were willing to fight and kill to protect my properties, but now that the law is more or less arriving in this part of the country, such men can become embarrassments. That's not to say that their occasional use may not be needed. But my point is they are tools of last resort. Why in God's name would I employ these men for the sole purpose of revenge? That would be a terrible waste of money and a risk not worth taking. I don't care if you live or die, but I'm not going to spend a single gold piece to decide your outcome."

McKenna was making certain sense, and he did not seem to be aware of Josh's relationship with Quanah—and why would he care? Comanche peace would probably be in the old rancher's best interest. "For sake of argument I'll accept that you're not trying to have me killed. Any suggestions on who might?"

"If it's not revenge or sudden anger, it's usually money. Are you engaged in a case that might affect somebody's money flow? If so, find out who that somebody is and you might find the would-be killer."

"That's not an easy task, but your suggestion is so obvious, I've been looking past it. I thank you for your insight."

Without another word, McKenna rose and walked away,

leaving Josh to ponder their strange meeting. He was inclined to believe the man, and Josh's suspicions had no doubt found their way to the older man who had a spider web network of information sources threaded through the Santa Fe community. It seemed highly unlikely that McKenna would have confronted him this way if he had been behind the attempts on Josh's life.

Josh gazed at a painting of an old Spanish mission that hung on the plastered restaurant wall, sipping on the remains of his bitter, black coffee. Who had something to lose from Quanah negotiating an honorable and profitable peace? Another thought occurred to him. How did the person or persons learn of Josh's association with the famous Comanche war chief? How did they learn of Josh's last mission on the Staked Plains and the timing of it?

25

TABITHA RIVERS HAD stacked a few larger stones to form a rough seat and now sat drowsily next to a sputtering, dying campfire. White Wolf sat across the fire from her, a haze of smoke drifting upward and nearly screening off his face from her view.

They were bivouacked with a force of some two hundred fifty mixed cavalry and infantry troops somewhere on the southern edge of the Staked Plains. It had been nearly three weeks since she covered the aftermath of Adobe Walls, and there had been no further encounters with hostiles. *The New Mexican* was forced to make do these days with little features about the sixty-year old sergeant who had been serving in one army or another for forty-four years or the boy-soldier who was one of thirteen brothers—a baker's dozen—to serve in the U.S Army. Tabby itched for a real story, and she vowed she would ferret one out soon.

Since the near-massacre, White Wolf had never been far from her side when he was in camp. He would go out on his scouting forays when ordered, but when he returned, he remained within easy calling distance. At night he spread his bedroll at a discreet distance but near enough to remain within her line of sight. She supposed he saw himself as her protector, and while she felt no particular fear, she could not deny she took some comfort from his presence.

Several evenings she had invited him to join her with some of the male reporters at her fire. The others did not protest because White Wolf usually gathered the firewood, which was scarce out on these plains, and brought in game to supplement the boring, if not disgusting, army rations. After the others drug their weary bodies to their blankets, Tabby had tried to engage in trivial conversation with White Wolf but with nominal success. She knew that he was fluent in her language, but he never initiated conversation, and his answers to her queries were unfailing brief and without emotion. She had yet to see him smile or hear him laugh. He was irritatingly calm and unexcitable whatever the seeming crisis. He had taken stoicism to a high art form, she thought.

She speculated White Wolf carried a story worth retelling, but she was going to have to extricate it like a skilled surgeon. She had no doubt that, sooner or later, she would. That was the foundation of her writing skills. A lot of people could put interesting words to paper. But the key was finding the story.

She looked across the smoldering embers. "Isn't this a strange place to camp?" she asked. "It's so flat you can see for miles. The Comanche can't miss seeing us."

"We can see them, too, if they approach. It would be foolish, with a force this size, to think the Comanche don't know where we are at every minute."

"Then why do we use such a huge force? Wouldn't it make sense to break up into a number of smaller units?"

"That is not for me to say."

"But you're thinking it."

He shrugged.

She shifted the subject, sensing he might be open to talking this evening.

"May I ask where you learned to speak English?"

"I have always spoken English."

"What do you mean?"

"I know that it might seem strange to you that a savage speaks your language, but many Cherokee have been bilingual for several generations. Unlike most Indian tribes, we have a written language and an alphabet, and whites have lived among our people for years . . . your famous Sam Houston among them. I attended a Quaker school where only English was spoken."

He was speaking with some pride, she sensed, and there was a teacher within him who sought to dispatch her ignorance. She recognized this as a key moment on the road to satisfying her journalist's curiosity. "I never thought of you as a savage. But I have never encountered a man of your heritage who was so fluent. Actually, you make me feel incompetent. I have lived among Spanish people most of my life, but I only know some common phrases to allow me to get by."

He remained silent.

"If I angered or hurt you, I apologize."

"You speak of my heritage. I think of myself as Cherokee, but my father's father was a Scottish trader. My mother is half Tonkawa. Rattlesnake is my cousin."

"How did you end up here?"

"The money. I was riding to Santa Fe and stopped at Rattlesnake's village. I had no money, and Rattlesnake told me the army was recruiting scouts for the coming campaign. I had military experience, of course, and saw no reason why I couldn't be an adequate scout, so I signed up with Rattlesnake, and we were fortunate to be attached to the same unit."

"May I ask why you were going to Santa Fe?"

"I am intrigued by the mingling of cultures there, but I also thought the Spanish architecture was suited to my skills. I am a carpenter and a mason, and I build things. I also dabble with sculpture and painting, and I thought I might find a market for my work."

Tabitha found herself speechless for several minutes before she spoke. "This is all very bizarre, you know . . . an Indian scout who plans to set up a business in Santa Fe. You would make a great story."

"No story."

"But—"

"No story."

The tone of his voice warned her not to pursue the issue for now. But the seed was planted, and she was already writing the feature in her head. She had hundreds of questions, and, sooner or later, she would, sliver by sliver, pluck the answers from him. She changed the subject. "Are you and Rattlesnake riding out tomorrow?"

"Yes."

"I'd like to ride with you and see what you do. It would be a viewpoint probably never covered in a newspaper."

"For a reason. The entire purpose of a scouting mission is to find clues and signs of what your enemy is doing without being discovered. Rattlesnake and I never remain together when we ride into the enemy's territory. One can move about unseen where several can be sighted with less astute eyes. Another person with us would be a distraction . . . and a danger."

"Your answer is 'no' then?"

"I cannot make myself clearer." He got up and walked away from the smoldering coals.

Tabitha's eyes followed White Wolf's every step as he emerged from the smoke, pausing at the taut muscles of his buttocks and naked thighs that received only token cover from his loin-cloth. He was tall and lean and undeniably handsome. She wondered if the images that drifted through her mind now would be considered perverted. Certainly her father would have been disgusted by the thought of her lying with an Indian.

26

A FEW DAYS after Rattlesnake and White Wolf left the encampment on their scouting missions, Rattlesnake returned and reported directly to Colonel Miles, who was in command pending the arrival of General Mackenzie. Even though his permanent generalship was still making its way through military and civilian bureaucracies, most soldiers referred to Mackenzie by his brevet rank, although he was technically, like Miles, a colonel. Miles was not above correcting the record if a soldier misidentified Mackenzie's rank in his presence.

Less than an hour after Rattlesnake's report to Miles, Tabitha noticed activity at the far side of the camp and hurried to see if there might be a story in the making. As she approached, she could see that approximately twenty buffalo soldiers from Mackenzie's Ninth Cavalry were readying their mounts. The buffalo soldiers, so named by plains Indians because of hair that resembled the thick, kinky hair of the bison, comprised all-Negro units that Mackenzie had honed into a respected fighting force, renowned for ferocity in facing the enemy.

Tabitha approached Sergeant Zeke Hooper, a massive, muscular former slave with flawless, ebony skin. She had befriended him early on and had written a story about his tragic history, which included a forced separation from his wife and two sons because of his being placed on auction and purchased by an Alabama plantation owner who took him far from Hooper's native Georgia. Hooper had searched for his family after the war but they had disappeared into the wave of black exodus that followed the freeing of the slaves. According to Hooper, his sale had been triggered by his spurning of advances by his master's wife, who subsequently, in her anger, claimed he had made the overtures. He had shown Tabitha the crisscrossed scars of the whip lashes on his back that had resulted.

Hooper was adjusting the saddle on his sorrel gelding when Tabitha came up behind him. "Zeke, where are you headed?" she asked.

Hooper turned, and when he saw her, smiled broadly. "Why, Miss Tabby, I ain't seen hide nor hair of you since we set up camp at this godforsaken place. Where you been keeping yourself?" His voice was deep and almost melodic like gently rolling bass drums.

"I've been tracking down stories."

He nodded his head knowingly. "And you all think you've tracked one down here?"

"Have I?"

"Depends."

"What does that mean?"

"Depends on what we runs into out there." He waved his arm toward the southwest. "Seems that Rattlesnake caught sight of some of them folks we been looking for. Little war party . . .

dozen or so perched and waiting down by a place called Dry Creek that ain't so dry right now. Looks like they're waiting to join up with another bunch. About three miles from here. Colonel thinks we should show the big chiefs what we do with these varmints. Rattlesnake, he not too sure about this. Worried that others might show up."

"But you're going after them?"

"Seems so. Yes, ma'am."

"Can I ride along?"

Hooper's eyes widened. "No, Miss Tabby. I don't thinks so. There's likely going to be serious shooting and hand-to-hand. Too dangerous. Besides, I got no say-so with you news folks. Somebody up the ladder gots to do that. Not me. No, ma'am."

"If Colonel Miles approves, can I ride with you?"

He shook his head in disbelief. "I got no say. But I think Colonel Miles say it's a bad idea."

Tabitha wheeled and raced to the other side of camp where she quickly gathered up her saddle, rifle, and other gear. Retrieving Smokey from the remuda was another matter, however. The hobbled horse was near the center of the herd, and Tabitha had to push her way through the jumble of grazing mounts in order to capture him and then repeat the task to lead him back out of the maze.

By the time her gelding was saddled—and she was ready to ride—Hooper's buffalo soldiers were a lingering cloud of dust in the southwest. So she urged her mount forward and began to chase the cloud.

Several miles out, she determined she was steadily gaining on the troops, and she figured she should catch up with them in another fifteen minutes. Then, suddenly, she caught a glimpse of a dark rider with a menacing, painted face angling toward her from her right. She started to veer to her left before she saw three Comanche warriors closing in on that side. All she could do was to forge straight ahead and try to outrace the marauding killers and reach the troops. It was possible, she thought. She would weigh less than any of her attackers, and she had yet to see a faster horse than Smokey given full rein. "Ride with the wind, big guy," she whispered, as her horse lunged forward.

She was pulling well ahead of her pursuers when she caught sight of a swarm of Comanche ahead of her, not coming her way, but evidently attacking the soldiers from the rear. If she kept on riding, she would end up in the middle of the war party. She tugged lightly on Smokey's reins, tossed her head over her shoulder and looked back. The Comanche to her right was nearing, but he was only one, she concluded. The others, yelping enthusiastically like hounds chasing a rabbit, were three. She swung right, hoping to sweep past the oncoming horseman and win a race back to the encampment. That was before the stone end of a war club crashed into the side of her head and launched her off of her racing horse.

27

THE FOUR RIVERS brothers and their father, Levi, sat at a rectangular pine table in The Exchange Hotel's dining area. The elder Rivers, by virtue of ingrained habit, was seated at the head of the table. It was the morning of Cal's wedding, which was to occur mid-afternoon, and the males had been pushed out of the way while the ladies finished wedding preparations, not that there were any protests at this table.

As the men launched their attack on breakfast, Levi, a barrel-chested man in his mid-sixties, whose face was sun-bronzed with sharp crow's feet lines carved in the flesh about his eyes, lamented, "I wish your little sister would have made it back for this occasion. She's always off to hell and gone someplace. Never thinks of her family."

"Pop," Josh said, "Tabby didn't even know about the wedding. This came up pretty fast. And she's like everybody in the family . . . she's got work to take care of."

"Work. Writing stories. Hell, what kind of work is that?"

Hamilton, the banker son, defended his sister, "Important work, Pop. Her stories for *The Santa Fe New Mexican* are being reprinted all over the country. I doubt if she's making more than a pittance now, but when she gets back, she'll have some leverage and probably even be in demand on the speaker's circuit. I've read her stories. I promise she's better than good."

"Yeah, I know, she writes okay, but she's going to get herself killed or end up some buck's squaw. She ought to have a husband by now . . . with a baby on the way. But never mind, you boys always stood up for your little sister no matter what she done. I'm not going to get anyplace with this bunch."

Josh conceded his father was right on that point. Tabby had been spoiled rotten by the brothers, and she'd always tagged along as part of the gang. But she learned a lot of skills and acquired a lot of toughness along the way that he hoped would help her now out on the Staked Plains.

"I'm getting married, too," Levi blurted out.

Heads turned, and uplifted coffee cups and forks froze in place at the words.

"What's everybody looking at? I just thought you might want to know."

"Dawn?" Josh asked.

"Who the hell else do you think it would be? We've been keeping company for a year now."

Dawn Rutledge was Erin McKenna's aunt, who had been living with Erin at the time of her capture by the Comanche. Dawn had employed Danna Sinclair and, ultimately Josh, to abort the lawsuit by Erin's uncle, Oliver McKenna, to have Erin declared dead and Oliver adjudged as the sole surviving heir to her father's vast ranch holdings. In the course of the trial and search for Erin, Dawn Rutledge had been invited as a guest at the Slash R, and Josh had no doubt she was sharing his father's bedroom by now. This was fine as far as he was concerned. She was a quiet, thoughtful woman, who seemed to have a calming effect on his father, who leaned toward the excitable.

"Congratulations, Pop," Josh said, standing and reaching across the table to shake his father's hand. The other brothers followed suit.

"She's a fine woman," the soft-spoken Nate said. His blessing counted most, Josh thought. Nate, physically a younger version of his father, and the eldest Rivers son, lived with his wife and three children in another house on the Slash R. He was a shy, quiet man who knew cattle and ranching and pretty much ran the spread. He never fought with Levi like some of the others had. He had a knack for knowing when to take good advice and when to let Levi's words go in one ear and out the other.

Ham said, "And when's the big day?"

"This afternoon."

This got Cal's attention. "But I'm getting married this afternoon."

"Well, the good preacher's going to tie the knot for Dawn and me after you're all hitched."

"I never heard of such a thing," Cal said.

Josh and his other brothers looked on with amusement. Ham asked, "Pop, does that mean Cal calls you 'uncle' now?"

Cal's eyes shot sparks at Ham. "Now, what in the hell do you mean by that?"

"Dawn is Erin's aunt. So, as I've got it figured, when Dawn marries Pop, he becomes Erin's uncle as well as her father-in law. It seems to me, then, that Pop's sort of your uncle, too."

"Can't be. Shit. Pop, you've got to re-think this. This seems like some kind of sick stuff."

"I've done my thinking. The deal's all but sealed."

"Why didn't somebody tell me about this? It's my wedding."

"Dawn talked to Erin, and she thought this was a great idea. Erin wanted it to be a surprise."

"Well, it sure as hell is that. I like Dawn just fine, but—"

Josh interrupted. "Cal, don't worry about it. This is all legal and moral, and we can make you and Pop both honest men in one sweep."

Cal seemed mollified but pushed his plate away and leaned back in his chair, shaking his head and mumbling to himself.

Josh turned serious. "There's one other thing I'd like to bring up while we're all together. I just felt you should know there have been some developments concerning Michael."

Josh had their attention. He told them about Clayborne Pierce's efforts to ransom Michael and the frustrating outcome. "It's almost certain Michael's with Quanah's band. Cal is aware I have spoken with Quanah and have contacts there, but it appears they have outright lied when I've inquired about Michael. We know with near certainty where he's at. And after this wedding I intend to bring him home."

Levi spoke with tears glazing his eyes. "Son, I'm overwhelmed at the prospect of Michael coming home. That's been my dream for some four years now, but you ain't just going to amble in there and tell Quanah to turn over that boy. Not if you want to walk away with your scalp."

"No, I'm working on some legal matters that are important to Quanah, and I'm not without leverage to broker a deal."

Ham said, "If you need money for ransom, it can be arranged."

Nate spoke. "I'll say what Pop might say if it wasn't for

worrying about what I'd think. The Slash R's never got cash, but we're good to borrow whatever we need to get your little boy home. This is family, and we stick together." Those words constituted a major speech for Nate, who was inclined to three to five word dialogue.

"I appreciate that you've offered to help, and I won't hesitate to come with my hat out if I need that kind of support. I can't put my finger on what it is yet, but I think this is about something other than money."

Cal had remained silent while Josh related what he had learned about Michael's captivity but now spoke. "When are you leaving?"

"In a few days. I have a few things to take care of at the office first."

"I'll be riding with you."

"Don't be ridiculous."

"I've scouted that country. That's what I did before I got domesticated."

"In a few hours you'll have a wife. Willow's as much your child as Erin's, and in a month you'll have another. You've got responsibilities."

"Yes, I do. And you and Michael are included."

"What the hell will Erin say about this? You get married and then you're off to Comanche country."

"I'll talk to her, but she won't fight it. I'm marrying her because I know the kind of woman she is."

Josh said, "Talk to her. Then decide."

28

AFTER THE DOUBLE wedding the Rivers clan gathered at The Exchange again. There was no ballroom, but a section of the dining room had been cordoned off for the wedding guests, which consisted mostly of family, Josh's law partners, Jessica, and a few of Levi's old friends who lived in Santa Fe. Cal had always been a loner and his few good friends were fellow scouts who were out on the plains with duties connected with the Red River War.

The exchange of vows by Levi and Dawn Rutledge had been a mere footnote to the wedding and had not overshadowed the main event by any means. After the minister had completed the ceremony for Cal and Erin, and their recessional was concluded, he simply asked the attendees to remain seated and called the older couple to the front. In a few minutes another married pair emerged from the church.

A mix of Mexican and American foods were spread out on the tables, and the guests grazed at their leisure. Josh, as best man for Cal, offered a toast to a "happy and enduring marriage and patience for the bride." He wondered if Cal had told her yet. Her flame-red hair glowed against a fashionable emerald gown. She had dismissed traditional white as an option. Her enormous belly and the beautiful half-Comanche toddler belied any notion she might be a virgin. She was a stunning young woman, Josh thought, and tough and smart—a good match for Cal.

Levi and Dawn sat at a table with Nate and Julia and their kids. They seemed quietly happy. He guessed Dawn was probably ten years younger than his father, and she was certainly an attractive woman. He was pleased for his dad. It was time to move on—for Levi. He was surprised at how much Nate's children had grown, but Eli, the older of the two boys was probably twelve now. That would make Levi II nine and Katherine about five, nearly the same age as Michael. Julia, with her honey-colored hair and full figure was aging well, he thought, and then he remembered she was likely not yet thirty-two. She probably would not have appreciated his thought.

"Good evening, counsellor." He turned at the sound of the familiar voice,

"Danna. I'm glad you could join us."

"You seemed very preoccupied."

"Just looking over the family. It's been a long time since this many of us have been together at the same time."

"It's got to be special."

He remembered that Danna had no family remaining, and he suspected she and Cal had once been lovers. This night was probably not that uplifting for her, but you would never know it by the happy mask she wore on her face.

"Can we talk a little business?"

"I'm heading out to look for Quanah's village day after tomorrow."

"I assumed it would be soon."

"I want you to tell George Hatter I'll be leaving in a week."

A look of puzzlement crossed her face. "I don't understand."

"I suspect someone in our office is the source of information about my travels and the fact we've been representing Quanah. Linda? No. I'd bet my life on it. Marty is new here. But let's keep this between you and me. Watch George and try to tell if he has any reaction to my leaving early. Maybe the suspicion isn't warranted."

"But why?"

"Money. There's an old saying that 'government is where the money is.' Government policies concerning the Indians affect some businesses and certain bureaucrats whose interests are either harmed by peace or the type of peace that is negotiated. Just keep an eye on George."

"I will, but it's difficult to believe he would be involved in anything like that."

Their conversation was interrupted by a breathless towheaded boy of about fourteen. "Mr. Rivers?"

Josh turned to the boy. "I'm Josh Rivers."

"I'm Danny Hicks. My father's the news editor at *The Santa Fe New Mexican*. He said I should deliver this to you right away." He thrust an envelope in Josh's hand and disappeared.

"What could this be about?" Josh muttered as he opened the envelope and plucked out a single sheet of paper. He read it with disbelief. "Oh shit," he whispered as he passed the note to Danna.

"Oh my God." Danna read aloud. "Josh Rivers. I regret to inform you that we have received a missive stating that your sister, Tabitha Rivers, is missing following a Ninth Cavalry engagement with hostile Comanche. We will notify you immediately if we receive further information. I trust you will notify appropriate family members. Regards, Elmer Hicks."

Danna returned the note. "What are you going to do?"

"Find her. And I'm afraid I'm going to throw a big bucket of water on this wedding party."

29

WHEN WHITE WOLF returned from his scouting assignment, Major Clinton Garden, Colonel Miles's second-in-command, informed him of the Comanche ambush of the buffalo soldiers and that Tabitha Rivers had either accompanied the troopers or been on her way to joining up with them. Miles added meaningfully, "She left without authorization, and as a result the shit is going to fly. She's become very popular in the public eye. Many people see the war through her words, and when news gets out she's been killed or captured, there will be a public outcry. Frankly, she's a foolhardy little bitch as far as I'm concerned."

White Wolf subdued his initial instinct to flatten the pompous weasel's turned-up nose. Instead, he asked, "How many casualties?"

"Eight dead, seven wounded. Three are missing, including Sergeant Ezekiel Hooper, and not counting Miss Rivers. Hooper was in charge, and I'll have his black balls for allowing that female correspondent to go with him."

If the Comanche haven't already taken them, White Wolf thought. "Where was the attack?" he asked.

Garden pointed to the southwest. "See those chimney-like rock formations in the distance? Just a bit beyond that. Near enough that we could hear the gunfire. Colonel Miles sent reinforcements, but it was a quick hit and they were gone. Like goddamn ghosts."

"I would like to take a look."

"Go ahead. I can't see that it would do any harm. If you find that woman, drag her ass back here."

White Wolf did not mention that he did not plan to return without Tabitha. He made a quick stop at the quartermaster's tent for a few supplies and then swiftly rode out of camp.

An hour later he was at the site of the attack. He could tell the Comanche strategy had been simple—the element of surprise, primarily. No attack had been anticipated this close to the main encampment, and the Comanche, evidently with as many as fifty warriors, had split their numbers, with about half remaining hidden as the troopers passed by and the others mounting a frontal attack. After that, like pincers, the Comanche closed in from behind, and they had the soldiers trapped in between. If not for the proximity of the main force, the entire squadron would have been dead and scalped. White Wolf guessed this was Quanah thumbing his nose at the white eyes.

He made a wide circle of the area and confirmed there were no other bodies left behind. He also determined that the body of warriors had split into three groups and moved out in different directions. Which should he track? He decided it didn't matter. They would probably join up at an appointed rendezvous or the same village anyway, so he picked the middle trail.

It quickly became evident the Comanche were making no effort to hide or cover their trail, and they were moving at a leisurely pace, evidently unworried about pursuit—or welcoming it. The latter was more likely, he figured. Chances were an unpleasant greeting lay ahead if the army took up the chase. It puzzled White Wolf they had not. If Mackenzie had been there, the troops would not have been frozen by command indecision and would have taken to the field.

He had to assume he was already being watched, so he was not going to surprise the war party. And what would it accomplish if he did, but his own death or worse? With that thought he angled away from the trail. He knew the general direction the Comanche were heading. There was no particular urgency. Either Tabitha was dead or she was a captive. If the latter, his first task was to locate her.

30

WHEN TABITHA AWAKENED, she found herself staring at the dry earth, rolling like a flowing river. Or it seemed it was moving anyway. In fact, she soon realized, she was slung over the saddle on Smokey's back like a sack of grain, her wrists anchored to her ankles by braided rawhide strips passing under the horse's belly. She felt like tiny spikes were being driven into her skull, and now she caught a glimpse of her own blood dripping intermittently on the ground beneath her. Turning her head, she saw that her gelding was being led by a mounted Indian—Comanche, she assumed.

It was nearing dusk, so she decided she must have been unconscious for some hours. She remembered racing to catch up with Sergeant Hooper's soldiers, but she could not recall anything beyond those moments and had no idea how she ended up face down over her horse's back. Out of the corner of her eye she caught a glimpse of a narrow ribbon of water winding its way through naked prairie that was turning more rugged as the terrain inched steeper now. The horses slowed and then came to a halt. She could hear her captors, obviously debating something in guttural voices, and then one voice rose above the others and uttered what she took as a command.

A warrior with a heavily painted face and a sleeveless, buckskin war shirt walked up to her, clutched her short-cropped hair and raised her head. Her gaze met his glaring obsidian eyes, and he let her head drop. He untied her wrists, and then grabbed her arm and pulled, flinging her harshly onto the ground. She landed on her shoulder and felt the shock jolt up her neck to her aching skull. She lay there motionless, taking in the scene, while the Comanche seemed to be tending to the tasks of setting up a night camp, ignoring her for the moment. She calculated there must be fifteen warriors, more or less. She lifted herself upon one elbow and scrutinized the site more thoroughly before her eyes fastened on the three blue-clad soldiers huddled together some forty feet from her and away from the bustle of camp activity. She could see they were bloodied, and it was easy to make out the bulky form of Sergeant Ezekiel Hooper. Though he was a fellow captive in a seemingly hopeless circumstance, his presence gave her a certain irrational comfort.

The warrior who had yanked her off the horse walked over and stood above her and glared. He said something unintelligible, but, from the tone, she knew it was not a friendly greeting. He kicked her sharply in the ribs, and she groaned as the blow sucked out her breath. Sour Face, as she thought of the scowling warrior, commenced waving his arms and growling at her, and she got the message she was to get on her feet. Slowly, she raised herself from the ground as a sharp pain ripped through her side, and she fought off dizziness that would sweep in and abate and then strike again. Finally, as she stood for a few moments, her head began to clear.

Sour Face grabbed her arm and dragged her away heading outside the edge of the campsite, and she followed, stumbling as she tried to keep up. He stopped abruptly and faced her. He signed clearly that Tabitha should remove her boots and britches. She felt the briefest wave of panic before resolve took over. She backed away, shaking her head from side to side defiantly. "No," she said. "No. Never."

He lunged for her and slammed a fist into the right side of her cheek, dropping her to her knees. Then he pushed her to the ground and bent over her and started pulling off her boots. She kicked and cursed, but soon he had removed them and commenced tearing off her trousers. She drove her knee upward with all the force she could muster and struck him solidly in the groin. She saw Sour Face double up in agony on the ground beside her and heard a small chorus of laughter nearby. Looking back toward the camp, she saw they had an audience of a half dozen warriors. She wormed away from her attacker and started running away from the camp, driven by instinct, knowing that her attempt to escape was futile.

Abruptly, an arm locked about her neck and jerked her to a stop. She was quickly released before a rough hand closed on her wrist and led back toward the camp. Tabitha could see Sour Face ahead of them, standing now with his hands on his knees, still trying to catch his breath. She studied her new captor as they walked. This warrior was a tall, lean and muscular man, by far the tallest Comanche in the war party, and his face was marked with only a few small streaks of red paint. They walked past Sour Face, whose eyes bored in on her with obvious hatred, no doubt, she thought, because of the humiliation in the presence of his tribesmen.

The Comanche pulled Tabitha along behind him until they reached a ragged deerskin spread out on the ground. "Down," he said.

She looked at him with astonishment. "You speak English?"

He did not reply to her question. "Down," he said, harshly this time.

She obeyed.

He turned away and seemed to be headed toward the other captives. The other Comanche had tethered the horses and now sat in little clusters about the campsite, seemingly no longer interested in her fate. The warrior who had placed her here was evidently someone of importance because Sour Face had not challenged him, and the others had shown him considerable deference. She wondered if she had now been claimed as his woman and whether she would soon be expected to submit her body to him. Her instincts readied her for another struggle, but her head told her it would be a hopeless battle with this man. He was an imposing figure, and she had no doubt she would ultimately surrender or die. She was a pragmatic woman, and she knew, in the end, she would choose to live.

Her eyes searched possible avenues of escape and found nothing. The landscape was all open country with no place to seek cover. There would be no river route to freedom this time, as she had seen warriors wading into the water and had noted the nearby creek ran no more than a foot or two deep.

Her head began to throb again, and dizziness overtook her. She lay back on the rough hide and drifted off to sleep. Darkness shrouded the camp when she awoke. She could still make out the shadowy movement of men moving about the camp and lumps of what she assumed were sleeping warriors lying on the earth.

Then she turned and saw the tall warrior sitting cross-legged not more than five feet off to her side, his eyes studying her with apparent curiosity.

He nodded at something next to her. "Water. Food."

She looked down and saw a military canteen and a chunk of some indeterminate substance within easy reach. She picked up the canteen, opened it, pressed it to her lips and had to restrain herself from downing the contents, realizing that her thirst was unquenchable. It occurred to her briefly that the canteen had probably been filched from some dead trooper. She plucked the other offering off the ground and examined it suspiciously. The contents seemed to be contained within a gut casing, almost like a sausage. She wondered if this was what whites called pemmican, which was said to be a mix of finely-shredded dried meat and melted fat with, perhaps, nuts and berries or any other convenient ingredients, depending upon the season.

Tabitha was suddenly starving and decided she didn't care what the Comanche might be feeding her. She squeezed the tube, and a mushy glob came out. Her fingers clasped it and pushed it into her mouth, and she began to chew. It was more than edible, not close to a steak at The Exchange, but not unpleasant and surprisingly sweet. She quickly devoured it all.

She had almost forgotten about the Comanche and cast a glance his way to find that he was still studying her like a specimen of some type, although his face, illuminated in a shaft of moonlight, betrayed faint traces of a tight-lipped smile. "Thank you," she said softly.

He showed no sign of understanding but replied, "Why ride soldiers?"

She guessed he wanted to know why she was with the army.

"I am a reporter. I write stories for a newspaper."

She saw his look of bewilderment. "I tell people in our villages about the war."

"Tell stories. Why woman?"

"Why not?"

"How you called?"

"You mean my name? I am called Tabitha Rivers."

He seemed agitated at her response. "Rivers?"

"Yes, Rivers. How are you called?"

He hesitated for some moments. "Me called Quanah."

Impossible, she thought. She had just stumbled onto the biggest story of her fledgling career—if she lived to tell about it. She was stunned nearly speechless to find herself in the presence of the notorious Comanche war chief.

Quanah tossed her an old horse blanket and then turned away and lay down. She guessed their conversation, such as it was, had ended.

31

JOSH AND CAL rode out of Santa Fe before dawn, Josh astride his buckskin gelding and Cal riding a black and white speckled Appaloosa stallion. Two pack horses trailed behind. Their gait was slow, and the brothers chatted as they moved southeasterly toward the Staked Plains, or Llano Estacado, as many of the Mexican populace referred to it.

"Is Erin upset about your coming with me?" Josh asked.

"Hell, no. The first thing she asked when she heard about Tabby was whether I was going after her. She expected no less."

"You have an understanding woman, considering you've got a baby on the way and all."

"I know that. I hope we can get back before the baby comes. Erin and her Aunt Dawn—I guess she can still be her aunt—are going to stay in Santa Fe until the baby's born. I think Pop's going to hang around, too, at least for a while. Remember, it wasn't that long ago Erin was living with the Comanche. She knows about rough times."

"Do you ever talk much about the time she spent in captivity?"

"Not a lot. I never ask, but every so often she'll pop up with a story out of the blue. With all the shit raining down all at once, I hadn't had a chance to tell Erin about Michael till after we got word about Tabby. There's something she told me I should pass on to you."

There was something in Cal's tone that caught Josh's attention. "What was that?"

"It seems there was a little boy about Michael's age with Quanah's band who didn't look like any Comanche she ever saw. His eyes were especially noticeable . . . brown with green flecks. Sound familiar? And rusty-colored hair. She wasn't very good with her Comanche and had to be damn careful about asking questions or she'd get a good beating. The boy's mother was at least part white, Erin figured. Dark . . . but not Indian dark . . . and her features were more white-like. The boy's father was a warrior by the name of 'Four Eagles.' Erin thought he was the natural father and assumed the kid's differences came from a part-white mother."

"Did she know the mother's name?"

"Well, that's what about strikes me dumb. I met her when we ransomed Erin. You know her. Name's 'She Who Speaks.' What do you think of that?"

Josh remained silent as he tried to come to terms with the wave of emotions sweeping over him. Anger and disbelief mixed with the joy that he may be close to finding his lost son. "I think She Who Speaks is a lying, treacherous bitch."

"Well, Josh, I understand how you feel. But you've got to put your feet in her moccasins. In her mind Michael . . . if the boy is Michael . . . is her son, blood or not. Willow isn't my blood child, but I'd lie in a second to keep somebody from taking her away.

Actually, I'd kill the bastard before I got to lying. Maybe you're lucky to have your scalp."

"This is a huge complication. I'm working for Quanah. Frankly, he's my client in negotiating peace terms. This woman is our go-between, you might say. How in the hell do I wiggle my way through this mess? Incidentally, She Who Speaks is also known as Jael Chernik. She was a captive, too. She doesn't carry an ounce of Comanche blood."

"Well, we're not going to find Quanah's bunch real quick. You'll have time to think this out. But on another tack, do you think Tabby might be in Quanah's camp . . . if she's alive?"

"I've thought a lot about that. The Kwahadi bands are the only Comanche that haven't made peace. If she's not in Quanah's village, he should know where she's at. She'd be somewhere among his people. I don't know. I hold out hope she's alive. She's smart as hell. If they didn't kill her early on, she'd figure out how to survive."

"Well, we've got to find them first."

"They'll probably find us."

32

Josh had been on target about George Hatter's behavior, Danna thought, as she leaned forward in her chair and tapped her fingers rhythmically on the desk as was her wont when she was perplexed about something. Hatter had been visibly upset when he learned a full day after Josh's departure that the senior partner would not be in the office, perhaps, for several weeks or even months.

He had moaned about Josh missing his appointments, Marty and Danna had already split up the client load. Most had become accustomed to Josh's absences. One had even jokingly asked whether there really was a lawyer Rivers. Hatter didn't share the client's sense of humor, and he had demanded a meeting with Danna. She was expecting him shortly.

There was a light tapping on her office door, before it opened.

"Come in, Mr. Hatter. And be seated."

Hatter came in and sat down. His round face had a ruddy caste, and he was sweating profusely. His thin lips were pursed tight in a grim expression. Danna decided to force him to initiate the conversation and remained silent.

Finally, he spoke. "Miss Sinclair, I have some grievances I feel I must raise."

"I see. Please tell me about your grievances. I make no promises regarding action, but I'll certainly listen to what you have to say."

"It's about Mr. Rivers and his lack of cooperation."

"I don't understand. He's not here all that often, and you do very little of his work. Linda handles most of his matters."

"But I deal with many of the clients who make appointments or ask about his work. I generally handle the management of the front office, and it's an embarrassment when I cannot account for his availability. I need to know when he's leaving and where he's going."

"With all due respect, Mr. Hatter, I don't think Josh Rivers needs to account to you on either of those issues. And if you have a disgruntled client, refer him to me. I'll address any concerns. I'm the managing partner. That's my job. With Martin Locke joining the firm, we can handle any of Josh's clients with little problem."

Danna could see scarlet creeping up the flesh of the law clerk's neck and into his cheeks. He was clearly angry and frustrated, but she was confident he was not willing to risk his job with intemperate statements.

"May I ask where Mr. Rivers is now and when you expect him back?"

"Not that I'm obligated to reply, but he and his brother, Cal, have ridden north to the Slash R, their father's ranch, to look over some property that may become involved in a land grant dispute. I expect him back within ten days," she lied.

"Levi Rivers and his new bride are still in Santa Fe, as is Calvin Rivers' wife, I'm informed. It seems strange that Levi, at least, did not join his son."

This man was certainly tracking the whereabouts of the Rivers family. "Well, Nate's family returned to the Slash R, and Nate runs most of the ranch business these days." She hesitated before continuing. "Now I have a question."

"Yes?"

"Why in the hell are you so interested in what the Rivers family is doing?"

Hatter seemed momentarily stunned and removed a handkerchief from his coat pocket and dabbed at his perspiring brow. "No special interest. I work for a Rivers, so people seem to just be inclined to share local gossip about family members with me."

"Very well. Let me just say that we suspect information is leaking from this office, and, further, that this has been related to the attempts on Josh's life. We are going to determine the source of the leaks, and when we do, we'll take appropriate action." She stood. "Good day, Mr. Hatter."

Hatter got up, and she could see he was confused about his abrupt dismissal.

"Yes, of course. I have some filings to make at the courthouse I must be taking care of."

Hatter escaped quickly through her office door and she followed him, meeting Marty Locke in the hallway. She saw George Hatter grab a few file folders and head out the office door. She nodded at Marty, and he returned the nod and moved toward the doorway that led to the Plaza.

33

MARTY GAVE GEORGE Hatter a healthy lead and angled across the street, thinking he would be less conspicuous trailing along on the opposite side. He was surprised, however, when Hatter made an abrupt turn and headed deliberately for the federal courthouse on Marty's side of the street. Fortunately, Hatter appeared focused on his destination and did not look Marty's way.

Marty did not entirely understand why he was following the law clerk. He had been told only that Danna suspected the employee of leaking important information from the firm—information that literally meant life or death. He was dubious that the suspicion would be confirmed this day since Hatter seemed to be going right to his stated destination. Marty decided to follow Hatter into the building. It didn't matter if he were seen here. As a lawyer it would not be unusual for him to cross paths with a law clerk in the city's hub of legal activity.

Marty saw Hatter disappear into the court clerk's offices just as he entered the courthouse hall. He had a case he could inquire about there, so, after a brief wait, he opened the door and walked in. He was greeted by three male clerks at their desks and a woman standing behind the long, ornate counter that separated the desks from the receiving area. But George Hatter had disappeared.

Marty gave Tara Cahill, a petite, attractive auburn-haired woman, his most charming smile. "Good morning, Tara. How's your day going?"

She smiled back. "Hi, Marty. Things could be worse. Judge is in, though, so we have to be on our toes."

Judge Andrew Robinson had a reputation for impatience and arrogance, and he supposed staff didn't mind his being tied up in court or, even better, at home on his little ranchero just outside Santa Fe. "Could I take a look at the Sanchez case file? I didn't write down the next court date when the judge held the motion hearing."

"Sure, I'll find it. Be just a minute." She turned away and went to a row of heavy cabinets that lined one wall.

Marty's eyes scanned the room. Two doors. One he knew to be a storage room and closet. The other had the words 'Judge Andrew Robinson' inscribed on it. George Hatter was meeting with the Federal Territorial Judge? That made no sense. Federal judges didn't confer with law clerks. Tara returned with a skimpy file folder. He pretended to peruse the judge's notes as he spoke softly to Tara, who was making entries in a ledger on the counter. "I could have sworn George Hatter was on his way over here."

Without looking up, Tara responded. "Oh, he's with the judge. They've been quite the chums this spring and summer. Your law clerk's a regular visitor. I'm surprised the judge doesn't insist that one of your lawyers handle all of your business before him. Of course, George has been clerking long enough he's close to a lawyer."

"He is that." Marty closed the file and moved along the counter to get closer to Tara. "Thanks, Tara." And then in a near whisper, he said, "Would you consider having dinner with me some evening?"

She looked up, her eyes seeming to study him suspiciously. "When?"

Marty shrugged. "Tonight?"

"So soon?"

"It doesn't have to be. You say when."

"Tonight would be okay. I live at Señora Munoz's boarding house. You may call for me there. Six-thirty?"

"I'll be there."

On his way back to the office Marty found he was surprisingly buoyant. Other than an occasional business lunch with Danna, he had not asked a young woman out since his arrival in Santa Fe. He felt a bit of guilt because the invitation was triggered by his search for information, but he also had thought on several occasions Tara was a woman he would like to know better.

34

"BEFORE WE ORDER, Mr. Locke, I would like to lay some cards on the table."

What was this about? She had been quite demure when she met him outside the boarding house, which was located only a few blocks from The Exchange. They had exchanged a few forgettable pleasantries on their stroll to the hotel's dining room, and she had been very soft spoken, seeming almost shy. And he had been staring at her unabashedly, he now realized, for in the course of abandoning her drab office clothing for a jade dress with a daring neckline, Tara had undergone a metamorphosis into a stunning young woman.

"Are you listening, Mr. Locke?"

"I'm sorry. I hope we can at least be on a first name basis."

"Of course, but I have something very serious to say."

"Yes, you were going to lay some cards on the table."

"I just wanted you to know that I'm aware you didn't invite me out because of my charming personality."

"Well, I don't know you well, but you've always shown a very friendly and pleasant personality when I've been in the court's offices. But, if I may be so bold, I think you are a very attractive woman, and I thought it would be nice to get to know you better."

She gave him an exasperated look. "You want to pump me for information about something. That was obvious today at the court. You have had ample opportunity to get to know me better. It's more than coincidence you asked me to dinner today. I just wanted you to know that we don't have to waste time playing games. You may ask your questions, and I will decide whether to answer. Now that's out of the way. I'm starved. May we order?"

She had left him speechless. Her coffee brown eyes were fixed on him now, obviously waiting for a reply. He signaled to the waiter. "Of course," he said. "I'm hungry, too. And I'll concede to an ulterior motive, but I hope we can enjoy each other's company a bit as well."

"We'll see," she said noncommittally.

They both ordered steaks and fried potatoes with apple pie for dessert. Marty noted Tara had a healthy appetite. While they ate, he steered the conversation to the mundane and was surprised to learn she already knew a considerable amount about him, including the fact that he had been a Confederate officer, was a University of Virginia graduate, and had lost a wife and child. "Court gossip," she had explained. "We know more about you than you know about yourself."

He learned she was an army brat, whose father, a now retired colonel, had been commandant at Fort Union before he returned to the East. Resisting her parents' protests, she had remained behind. She loved the Southwest, she had just turned nineteen, and she didn't deny that her father's influence had helped her find a position in the Territorial Court office. Her present work was temporary, as she hoped to carve out a future in some kind of business, yet to be identified.

After she took the last bite of her pie, Tara said, "Very good, Marty. Thank you. Now you may proceed, as the judge would say."

In spite of their uncomfortable beginning, Marty had found Tara to be an engaging and funny dinner partner. He hated to destroy the light mood that had eased its way into their evening. "I'm embarrassed that you caught me at my deviousness. But before I talk business, would you give me another chance? There is a play at the Teatro Santa Fe next week. Perhaps we could have dinner again and then attend the play."

"What if I get mad because of the questions you're going to ask me?"

"Then I'll hope you forgive me and accept my invitation anyway."

She smiled mischievously. "You can be charming. I'll accept . . . tentatively."

"Very well. I'm going to gamble that you will be discreet about our conversation"

He explained about the suspicions of his partners regarding George Hatter's behavior. "I haven't been with the firm long enough to be privy to all the details, but Danna seems to think this leak has a relationship to attempts on Josh's life."

"I don't see what this has to do with Judge Robinson."

"I admit it seems difficult to make a connection, but you say Hatter's been visiting the Judge regularly?"

"At least weekly for the last three months or so. They often will be together for as much as an hour."

"What do you think of Judge Robinson?"

"I think he's a pompous ass. I'm not fond of him. He's made advances to me on several occasions . . . brushing his grubby hands against my breasts, patting my bottom, that sort of thing. Never overt, but I know it's not accidental. He scolded me once about not being friendly, whatever that means. I'm the only female in the court's offices, so I'm his only target, I guess. He is engaged, you know?"

"Yes, Constanza Hidalgo. She comes from a prominent Spanish ranching family, as I understand it."

Tara hesitated. "I'm going to sound like an old gossip, but I don't know if you're aware of something."

"What?"

"Constanza was once Josh Rivers's lover. It was assumed by many they would be married."

"I wasn't aware of that. I suppose that would not endear him to the judge."

"Not likely."

"My guess, though, is that money is at the root of this. I can't see where the judge would be profiting from any information Hatter would be feeding him."

"Judge Robinson conducts a lot of non-judicial business from his office. He seems to have a lot of financial interests. Bankers and local ranchers and businessmen call on him all the time." She frowned and was silent for some moments. "There is someone else who is a frequent visitor."

"Yes?"

"Simon Willard. He's the General Procurement Officer for all of the military operations in the Southwest. He's not uniformed or anything, so I suppose he's civilian. Tall, skinny guy that looks like a starved hound. He's always wearing a different suit when he comes in, boots perfectly clean and polished . . . how he does it when we walk in nothing but dust and horse dung around here, I don't know. He shows up every few weeks, and sometimes he'll spend several hours with the judge. Now if I wanted to play detective that's somebody I'd take a look at."

"And I suspect we will. I can't thank you enough for your help. Do I still have standing to take you to the Teatro?"

"I think you have that much standing."

"Then I'm forgiven?"

"No, but you're making progress."

35

THE SUN HAD crawled half way across the cloudless skies, and its searing rays were filtered only by a few scrub willows and cottonwoods clinging to the banks of the near-dry creek bed that wound around three sides of the temporary village. She Who Speaks, formerly Jael Chernik, sat in front of her tipi, her son, Flying Crow, facing her and sitting only a few paces away, fidgeting impatiently while they went through his English lessons.

He was a Comanche boy through and through, and the mother knew she could not make a five-year old understand why he had to undergo these daily exercises where he learned new words from another language and was allowed to speak only English for several hours at a time. And twice a week they went through the same process with Spanish. She did not think she was deluding herself when she concluded he was extremely bright and quick. She thought he had her natural affinity for languages, but she reminded herself that it could not have been inherited from her. Nonetheless, it pleased her greatly and she was confident it would stand him in good stead in the new world that was on the horizon.

"Mother," Flying Crow implored, his green-flecked brown eyes pleading, "We are hunting buffalo today. My friends are waiting. May I go now?"

He had been reasonably patient, and he had put in his time. She smiled. "Go my little warrior and bring back much meat for our fire."

He leaped up and snatched his tiny lance and disappeared quickly in the dust. Soon, he and a half dozen other boys would be killing phantom buffalo and trying to convince some of the little girls to come and do the skinning. Let them savor the moments that remain, she thought. The end was near. No more than a year at most, and the Kwahadi would be trekking to the reservation. And then what?

She guessed there would be a concerted effort to repatriate white captives. Quanah would help her shield Flying Crow, but she doubted that would be enough. Someone would tell when it became profitable to do so, if it even came to that. Her husband, Four Eagles, had brought Flying Crow home from a raid when he was little more than a year old. She had not borne him any children, although he had three by his other two wives. She Who Speaks had been taunted subtly by the other wives for her failure to produce a child, mostly, she knew, because she was Four Eagles's favorite. She had been ecstatic when her husband presented her with the baby boy, who quickly became her life. Her affection for her husband had grown in response to the gesture, and she was more passionate in her lovemaking when he came more often to her robes during the hours of the night.

Her immediate concern was the boy's father. She had known instantly when she saw Josh Rivers's eyes. It was not just the distinctive hue and color, but the way they seemed to focus and burrow into one's soul. She hated that she had deceived Josh. She liked him and respected him and felt something more for him, although she could not have placed a label on it. She knew there would be hell to pay when he learned that Flying Crow had once been known as Michael Rivers. She truly hoped she did not have to kill Josh because, of course, she would if that was the only way to save her son.

There was a stirring in the sleepy village that quickly grew into a racket. She Who Speaks recognized the hubbub instantly. One of the war parties was returning. She hoped Quanah had returned with this one. The Comanche bands had multiple chiefs, but she was convinced that Quanah was the sole chief with sufficient versatility to bring the Kwahadi through this time and ultimately salvage a tolerable life for The People.

There seemed to be an unusual clamor, and, curious now, she got up and wound her way through the tipis, following the sounds of laughter and yelling. She stopped suddenly when she reached the mass of people surrounding Quanah and the war party, but her eyes quickly passed over Quanah and his warriors and froze on the bedraggled captives that trailed behind them. She saw a massive Negro trooper sitting erect in his saddle, his eyes defiant. The two other soldiers seemingly tried to shrink out of sight, and their faces betrayed terror. Rightly so, she thought sadly. At first She Who Speaks thought the other was a smaller white man, perhaps a civilian scout, but then she realized she was looking at a young woman attired in male garb. The woman seemed to be studying the village and its occupants with more curiosity than fear.

The soldiers and the woman were pulled off their horses, and the squaws and children and a few old men began beating on them with fists and sticks. A few had leather straps with which to administer their blows. The soldiers had their hands secured behind their backs and were helpless to defend themselves. The woman raised her arms to deflect blows from her face but refused to scream or cry, she noted. The beatings would not be life threatening. This was just entertainment, a showing of contempt for the captives. The poor devils would endure anguish they never in their worst nightmares would have dreamed of during the next few days, less if they were lucky.

Quanah caught sight of She Who Speaks and dismounted, and the Comanche taunters parted as he walked toward her. When he approached and stood before her, he towered over her. "Greetings, She Who Speaks," he said in Comanche. "You see there is a woman among the captives, and the others are of the buffalo soldiers. A strange collection of prisoners, are they not?"

"Yes, my Chief, but I think you must think very carefully about their fate."

"I have thought about the buffalo soldiers. They shall die screaming for their mothers just like the white eyes who have suffered Comanche deaths. But the woman is another matter. I have not yet decided. She is not a promising wife for our warriors. She is given to disobedience."

She decided now was not the time to open a debate with him about the torturing of the buffalo soldiers. "What was the woman doing with them?"

"At first I thought she was one of their whores who follow the camps. But she was armed and not dressed like I have seen these women. I tried to speak with her, but I did not deliver my words so she could understand them. One thing worries me."

"And what is that, my Chief?"

"I believe she told me her name is Rivers."

A shiver raced down her spine. "Do you think she is related to Josh Rivers?"

"I do not know. And if she is, I am uncertain what I shall do about it. I fear this is a captive we should have left behind. I want you to find out about this woman. Everything we should know."

She tossed a look back at the melee which seemed to be subsiding. The soldiers were blood spattered and the woman slightly less so, and the tormentors were getting bored. "If you will have someone bring her to my tipi, we will talk."

36

SHE WHO SPEAKS waited in her tipi for the mysterious white woman. The tipi walls had been rolled up several feet from the earth, and a nice breeze whisked through her living space and made the refuge from the sun comparatively comfortable. She pondered the conversation she would soon have with the woman. Female captives, of course, were not uncommon in Comanche villages, especially young ones selected by raiders for wives or slaves. But almost all were bounty from attacks on settlers or travelers. This woman, however, had a military connection of some kind, and Quanah had obviously identified her as someone who warranted scrutiny.

She heard a scuffle outside her entryway, and a moment later the white woman catapulted through the opening and landed face-down on one of the skins spread out on the floor. A warrior followed and asked if he should remain. She Who Speaks dismissed him and instructed him to wait outside and said she would call if she needed assistance. The woman was making no effort to get up, and her face and arms were smeared with blood and covered with welts. She did not appear a physical threat in her present state, and what would she escape to?

"Sit up while we talk, so we may see each other," she said softly but firmly. The body stirred and the woman turned her head toward the speaker who sat half a dozen feet away. The white woman's face was scratched and swollen, and she had a cut above her eye. She would look worse in the morning, but there was no reason they could not talk.

The woman twisted her body awkwardly as she drug herself to a sitting position, never taking her eyes off her host. She did not seem inclined to speak.

"I am She Who Speaks. Quanah has placed you in my custody for the time being. It is in your interest to answer my questions truthfully. Your life depends upon it."

"I can't think of any reason why I wouldn't answer truthfully. But I'm confused. You speak English perfectly and with no accent. Still you appear to be Comanche."

"I will ask the questions. What is your name?"

"Tabitha Rivers. My friends call me Tabby, but I guess we're not friends . . . yet."

She Who Speaks hoped she was not showing the anxiety she felt at the confirmation of the white woman's surname. "And where are you from?"

"Santa Fe. I'm a reporter for *The Santa Fe New Mexican*."

"A reporter? A writer for a newspaper? What are you doing in the middle of the Llano Estacado?"

"I am riding with the army as a civilian correspondent. I'm reporting on the Red River War."

"Red River War? A war? That's what the whites are calling the hundreds of soldiers in the field chasing ghosts?"

Tabitha returned a bitter smile. "The Comanche will not

always be ghosts. General Mackenzie is a seasoned ghost catcher. All that remain of the Comanche and Kiowa and other tribes of the southern plains are the Kwahadi band, and they are outnumbered by the American forces by more than ten to one. They will soon run out of places to hide, and if they do not make peace, they will be slaughtered and disappear like the buffalo."

She knew Tabitha Rivers spoke the truth. And Quanah had come to that realization as well. He was hoping to hold out long enough to negotiate favorable terms. "Your soldiers didn't fare so well against the Kwahadi or you wouldn't be here . . . along with the buffalo soldiers. The troopers will start the journey toward a terrible death tonight. You may go with them. That remains to be seen."

"If you torture and kill the soldiers, you will certainly have to kill me."

She Who Speaks was shocked at Tabitha Rivers's words, even more so at the matter of fact way in which she spoke them.

"I don't understand."

"Because if you allow me to live, someday I will write of the torture and killing of the captives. My stories appear in newspapers throughout the country. Do you think this will help the cause of the Comanche? Even if you kill us all, the Comanche will pay a huge price. I am the only woman war correspondent in the Southwest, possibly the first female battlefield reporter. My publisher has written that I am very well known . . . he says famous, but that's probably overstating it. Are you familiar with the phrase 'public relations'? It's a fairly new term."

Somehow this beat-up pup had taken control of the interrogation, but she was saying things that struck a chord within her. "Explain."

"Public relations are things that people do to make others look upon them favorably. This is something planned to obtain favorable results. Businesses might donate money to the poor or spend money for community projects, not necessarily because they want to be charitable, but because they want the public to look upon them with admiration or appreciation and, thus, be more inclined to patronize the enterprises. Politicians are constantly using public relations to curry favor . . . often by taking the money from the people and then giving it back to them in a way that the recipient thinks the politician has made a gift. The strategy is used very cleverly by some, and it may not always be done with honesty and sincerity, but it often accomplishes its purpose. And then there is the other side of that coin."

"And what is that?"

"Poor public relations. This happens when someone does something looked upon with contempt or disdain by others. If a merchant is known to beat his wife, other wives will likely avoid patronizing his store. It is not only wrong in our culture, it's not good business. A politician who is a drunk or who fails to show up on time for public events is also engaged in poor public relations and may jeopardize his election."

"I can understand that."

"And Comanche who torture and kill captives . . . particularly a well-known woman . . . are not setting themselves up for kind treatment by the politicians who will decide their fate. The politicians will find it good public relations to please their voters by punishing the Comanche."

"Everything you say is very self-serving."

"Of course it is. I want to live, and I want to write about this experience. My stories could be good public relations for the Kwahadi . . . if you think there is another side of the story to be told. Keep in mind that I am a reporter, and my first obligation is to report the truth as I see it. I will not write that cruelty is kindness."

She Who Speaks found the words of Tabitha Rivers very troubling. She guessed the white woman was about her own age, not much past twenty, but she was well practiced in cleverness and the skills of manipulation. And her words rang true. It was one thing to kill enemies in open warfare, but the killing of a female writer and torturing of captives, if it became known, would not advance the cause of the Kwahadi, but could Quanah prevent it even if he wanted? He was a war chief, one among at least four chiefs within the band. The decision would be made by a council of the chiefs and elders.

She decided she must ask the question she thought she knew the answer to. It could be important. "Tell me about your family."

Tabitha frowned. "What does that have to do with anything?"

"Tell me. Your life may depend upon it."

"That makes no sense. But all right, my father is a rancher in northeastern New Mexico. My mother was murdered by your brave Comanche warriors, along with my sister in law, whose baby was abducted by the same warriors and possibly killed. My brother, Nate, ranches with Pop. Brother Ham is a Denver banker, and Cal ranches now, too. My brother, Josh, whose wife your people murdered and whose son they stole, is a Santa Fe lawyer. Is that enough of my family history?"

She Who Speaks stared at Tabitha in disbelief. How could this be, that the Kwahadi war party could capture the sister of the lawyer who was to plead their case for favorable terms of surrender? And how would Quanah handle this when only a few like-thinking elders knew of his retention of a lawyer to assist with negotiations? She stood up. "You will remain here for now. I must speak with someone."

37

WHITE WOLF, FROM the rocky rim of a wide, shallow canyon had watched as the warriors moved their horses at a slow trot down the trail that cut between the steep walls. He had made a wide circle, stopping to rest his horse and sleep for only a few hours. Early that morning he had sighted a dust cloud crawling across the plains, and he had ridden ahead and found his hiding place above what appeared to be a well-used trail, and his judgment had been vindicated.

He had easily spotted Tabitha Rivers astride her smoke-colored gelding, and the bulky buffalo sergeant stood out like a big tooth among the riders. He determined there were three captive soldiers, and he had followed the war party at some distance. As expected, the Comanche who had split off following the successful attack gradually began to return and merge into the main party until once again they formed a substantial force. White Wolf kept his distance, knowing he could help no one if he were discovered. When he saw the tipis rising and spreading over the distant landscape, he reined his stallion away and sought out a place to hide and rest and think. After following a dry creek bed he came upon some seeping springs that offered both rider and horse a water supply after some digging with his hands.

He saw no sign that anything other than a few deer had been visiting the springs, and it afforded some natural cover with a scattering of large stones and brush. The location was a good five miles from the Comanche encampment, so he decided to settle in for a spell.

White Wolf staked out the stallion and dropped the saddle near a cluster of limestone rocks near the springs. He lay down, resting his head on the saddle seat, and promptly fell asleep. A few hours later, he woke up feeling energized and clear-headed and was ready to ponder the dilemma. It would be impossible, he thought, to accomplish a recovery of all the captives. His focus would be on Tabitha. Besides, he was forced to admit, her rescue had been his obsession from the beginning. They had become good friends in the course of their journey with the army, and, for his part, he realized now his attraction went beyond friendship,

First, he had to find her location within the village. He dug into his bedroll and removed a pair of faded denim britches and pulled them on. Then he stuffed the front pockets with cartridges for his Army Colt and Winchester. He also filled his army canteen from the spring and tied a little bag of deer jerky and crumbling, dry biscuits to his belt. Then he re-staked the stallion within reach of the spring, leaving the stake loose so the animal could pull free if he should be threatened by man or beast.

He did not like the prospect of being left horseless in this godforsaken country, but he could not just ride up to the camp like a cousin stopping by for a Sunday visit. He sat down again, and leaning back against a rock, he tugged his battered hat over his forehead and dozed off again. When he awoke this time, the sun was just beginning to creep behind the western horizon. He got up and began his walk in the direction of the village. It was turning dark by the time he got near the Comanche encampment, and a few fires were providing some light, but he had not figured out yet how he was going to find Tabitha, especially if she was confined to one of the tipis. He lowered himself to the earth when he was within a quarter mile and started crab walking. After finally snaking his way on his belly to the outskirts of the village, he watched and waited, first identifying the location of the horses. He would need mounts if they were to have any chance of escape, assuming he found her. He decided that stealing a few horses was the least of their worries, and Tabitha was a superb horsewoman, as good as anyone he'd seen, man or woman. They just had to make it to the remuda.

As the evening wore on, the village started to come alive. More fires erupted and a large blaze lit up an open area near the middle of the camp. A ceremonial fire of some kind, he guessed, and he did not think it portended well for the captives. Then he spotted Tabitha weaving her way through the village, talking animatedly with a Comanche woman.

He lay still, his eyes following the movement of the women until they stopped in front of a tipi, and the Comanche woman gestured for Tabitha to enter. She did without apparent objection, and the other woman followed. A half hour later, she exited, apparently leaving Tabitha alone. This was his opportunity.

38

THE MEETING WITH Quanah had not gone well. Tabitha had reason to think her own life had been temporarily spared, but the tribal council would decide the fate of the three buffalo soldiers. At most, she had purchased a few days' time with her plea for their lives. She Who Speaks had interpreted Tabitha's words with conviction, it had seemed. Tabitha was inclined to believe the Comanche woman had been persuaded to the view that something could be gained by foregoing the usual games with the captives. Quanah, however, had been unable to grasp the concept of a newspaper and the stories that were printed there, and his voice had turned sharp and anger had flashed in his eyes as She Who Speaks pressed him on the treatment of the prisoners.

The call for a council had been a small victory that was likely to be temporary. Maybe Mackenzie's cavalry would arrive to abort the torture given enough time. She could only hope. They sat in She Who Speaks's tipi now, the striking Comanche woman quiet and pensive. During their absence, as the sun had disappeared and the sky turned dark, a little, nearly naked, boy had slipped into the tipi and taken up a station as far away from Tabitha as possible. He sat on a buffalo robe glaring at her with suspicion, his hand clutching a sturdy stick that was no more than four feet long but with one end that tapered into a wicked point.

She Who Speaks, as if only now becoming aware of the boy's presence, turned toward him and, in Comanche, spoke softly and at some length. Tabitha gathered she was giving him some kind of assurance, but the boy did not respond and kept staring at her. She supposed this was the Comanche woman's son. Did that mean there was also a husband who would be sharing the sleeping quarters? Oh, God, She Who Speaks said Quanah had agreed to permit her to stay here. Had she unknowingly become some warrior's second wife? She had read and heard of the practice of polygamy among the Indians of the Great Plains and Comanche, in particular. She finally reminded herself that she was alive with some prospects of staying that way. She would endure what she must to see this adventure through. And that was how she saw life . . . a series of adventures, all fodder for good stories and, perhaps, someday a fantastic book, or two, or more.

She Who Speaks turned to Tabitha, "This is my son, Flying Crow. I explained that you are going to be staying with us and that he is to treat you with respect."

"He seems quite excited about the prospect," Tabitha replied sarcastically.

"He will become accustomed to it."

She decided to be bold. "Will his father object?"

"His father, Four Eagles, was killed by your soldier friends and now rides with his ancestors."

"I'm sorry. I didn't know."

"For now, you are here because I claimed you. It is my right as a widow and a counselor, so long as you do not become a problem for The People."

"Claimed me? What am I? Your slave?"

"You are whatever I choose you to be."

"I don't understand."

"Tribal custom dictated that I should become the fourth wife of my husband's brother when he was killed, but I chose not to . . . which was my right. Some have thought it strange that I did not choose other warriors who offered to take me and my son into their tipi. Rumors pass through the village that I am of two spirits."

"Two spirits?"

"Yes. That I would share a robe with one of my own sex."

Her words stunned Tabitha speechless.

She Who Speaks smiled for the first time since Tabitha had met her. "It is acceptable among the people, but it does not go unnoticed. Do not be concerned. I am not of two spirits. But if you choose to live, it behooves you not to discourage such thinking."

"You are one strange woman. Why are you helping me?"

"Because I think there was wisdom in your words when you suggested it might be wise to refrain from torturing and killing the captives. I would go a step further and take the buffalo soldiers to some distant place and set them free. Would that not be good public relations, as you say?"

"It would."

"And I do not find you too obnoxious. Perhaps, we can learn from each other."

"I would like to write. I had paper and pencils stuffed in my saddlebags. Do you think I could have them?"

"I see no reason why not . . . the paper and pencils, anyway, if they have not been discarded or burned. I have rarely had the opportunity to write, and I would like to refresh my skills."

"You can write?"

"Why not?"

"I don't know. You just confuse me."

"I shall explain in the days ahead, if I choose. Now I must speak with Quanah one more time, and I will see if I can determine what became of the saddle bags."

She Who Speaks got up and disappeared through the exit way, leaving Tabitha with the boy, who still watched her warily and silently.

39

WHITE WOLF HAD Tabitha's tipi pinpointed, and she was alone. He decided to do the last thing the Comanche would expect. He stood up and walked into the village just as if he belonged there, carefully weaving through the tipis and dodging in another direction when he saw an approaching man or woman. He consciously walked deliberately—a man on a mission, which, of course, he was.

When he reached the tipi, after a quick survey of the camp to confirm he was unobserved, he ducked into the entrance. "Tabitha," he whispered. "Tabby, it is White Wolf. Come with me. We must hurry." He saw her shadowy figure sitting no more than six feet away and reached out his hand, and then he saw she was shaking her head from side to side.

"No," she replied. "I think I am safe here. You must leave. If they catch you they will kill you in a terrible way. Go."

"I don't understand."

"Go."

Then a terrible pain struck him beneath his shoulder blade. He grunted with agony and heard something snap as he turned to face the source. He was disbelieving when he saw the little Comanche boy facing him defiantly with a broken stick in his hand. He grabbed the stick from the boy's hand and yanked it away, pushing the boy harshly and watching him hurtle backward before he landed on his butt.

"Run. I'm not going with you," Tabitha said, "I am not going with you."

He obeyed and tore through the tipi opening, racing through the camp, noticing out of the corners of his eyes that the few who saw him just looked at him curiously. And then the boy began to scream as White Wolf broke out into the open, running faster than he had ever moved in his life, the shooting pain on the right side of his upper back excruciating but not bringing him down. But every breath felt like he was being stabbed again.

He deviated from the direct route to his stallion, fearing that he would lead pursuers to his horse. His weapons and ammunition slowed him only slightly, and he hoped the calls of a small boy would not be immediately heeded. Also, the Comanche would not know whether there were others with him and would be likely to secure the perimeters of the village before sending a war party to find out what his appearance in the camp was all about.

When he reached the seeping springs, he was glad to see that his stallion, Storm, was still there. The horse whinnied and seemed to be welcoming him. White Wolf could feel his body weakening as he saddled the big stallion and knew his shoulder would be useless in a few hours. His only hope, though, was to put distance between him and the Comanche pursuers. He decided to head northwest in the opposite direction from which he had come, thinking they might expect him to backtrack to the military encampment.

He slowly lifted himself into the saddle and headed Storm at a breakneck pace. As he rode, he finally began to collect his thoughts and appraise his situation. The pain below his shoulder shot through his upper back with every rough spot on the trail. He was fairly certain the tip of the weapon—if that was what you would call it—had broken off with the impact of the thrust and was still imbedded in his flesh, but he could not reach the object in an effort to remove it. He did not think the little lance had driven deeply enough to strike any vital organs, but this would not prevent the wound from turning putrid and ultimately kill him.

But his embarrassment stung him almost as much as the wound. He had been taken down by a Comanche boy, who was no more than five or six years old. And, worse, he had made a foolish rescue attempt of a young woman, who obviously had no particular interest in being rescued and seemed even a bit annoyed at his effort. He wondered if there were opportunities for clowns in Santa Fe. Of course, the reality was that if the Comanche did not track him down, he was going to die somewhere out on this parched prairie, and the sun and the buzzards and other scavengers would make short work of him. He would disappear without a trace he had ever inhabited the earth.

The stallion raced on for some hours before he began to wheeze and blow. White Wolf knew that he had pushed the animal too hard and eased up. The Cherokee faded in and out of semi-consciousness and clung desperately to Storm's mane, and he had only a vague awareness of the stallion slowing to a walk. When he awakened, he found himself lying on his left side and his eyes squinting against the near-blinding rays of a sun that he figured was a few hours short of high noon. He suddenly realized he was stretched out on a blanket, and his head was partially resting on his saddle. The wound below his right shoulder throbbed and ached with some ferocity, but it was not nearly as painful as his last memory of it.

"Don't move." The voice came from behind him. The voice was soft with no edge of hostility.

A lean man with a black, short-cropped, full beard stepped around him and got down on one knee facing him. "You're looking some better," he said, "but you ain't out of the woods by a long shot. You speak some English?"

"Yes, I use that more than Cherokee anymore."

"Cherokee, huh? Knew a lot of them folks when I lived in East Texas . . . most of them on the Arkansas side of the line. Good people. Didn't think you was Comanche. I'm Charlie Goodnight, by the way."

"I am called White Wolf among my people."

"And when you're not among your people?"

"I have not decided yet, but I suppose I will adopt another name for convenience to assure some of the wary I am not a total savage."

"How about Oliver? Oliver Wolf? You keep a part of your people and take on a first name that couldn't be more English. Got to be honest, I'm taking the name from my late partner and the best friend I ever had, Oliver Loving."

"I'd be honored to carry your friend's name." Goodnight, Loving. The names had a ring of familiarity. Of course, he read of their exploits and heard tales of Charles Goodnight, some of which he doubted carried much truth.

"Now, Oliver Wolf, I will tell you what I know about your visit here, and then, since I've invested some time, I hope you let me in on your part of the story so I can find out if I need to get shored up for trouble. Your big stallion wandered into my campsite just before daybreak. He scared the living shit out of me, to be honest with you. But he was just looking for water and didn't seem to be shy about taking up with a stranger. I got a good spot for water and shelter here. Nice spring-fed creek, some undergrowth and trees . . . spindly as they are . . . and a rock wall that at least covers my backside. You were hanging onto the animal's mane for dear life but didn't seem to know it. I gave you a little tug and you slid off like a sack of feed, taking me down to the ground with you. You're a mite too big for me to handle."

"I don't remember any of this."

"That don't surprise me none. You couldn't make a sound beyond a mumble. Anyhow, I seen you had that bloody stick in your back, so I rolled you over on your belly and yanked the damn thing out. You bled like a stuck pig for a few minutes, but I figured that was good for cleaning out the wound. The bleeding eased up after a spell, and I poured the last of my whiskey in the hole. No great loss, since I'm not much of a drinking man anyhow."

"I'm obliged to you. I'd be a dead man if we hadn't stumbled into your camp."

"You still might be. You can't tell with wounds like these. You shouldn't move any more than necessary for a few days to keep the wound from breaking open. I could of done some stitches, but a doc told me once it was better not to close up these puncture wounds. Just let them air out and heal from the inside out. You'll have a nasty scar that looks like a puckered hog's butt.

I'd guess if it don't start to putrefy in the next few days, you'll likely make it. If the wound turns sour, there ain't much I can do but keep you company till it's over. That was a strange thing you had stuck in your back. How'd that come to be there, if you don't mind my asking?"

"Comanche." He gave a sheepish grin. "A five or six year old one. I think this was his lance." White Wolf told Goodnight the story of the ill-fated rescue.

"Do you think there's Comanche on your trail?"

"Your guess is as good as mine."

"I don't think they're looking very hard, or they would have caught up with you by now. You were smart to come this way. Their main worry would be that you were headed back to get the army. If they decided you didn't go that way, they might have lost interest a little quicker . . . but you never know with those devils. We'll keep an eye out. You know where we're at?"

"Somewhere on the Staked Plains, but that's the best I can do."

"We're on the southern tip of Palo Duro Canyon. It stretches for miles northwest from here and gets wider as you follow the creek. Grass and water. I'm fixing to stake out a big cow ranch here. The Comanche wars are about over, and I'm scouting out the canyon. This is the Comanche's favorite stomping grounds, but they've been hit by the army in the canyons several times recently, so I don't think they'd be moving the main body this way right now. If they do we'll beat the hell out of here."

"You're the Charles Goodnight who served with the Texas Rangers, I assume."

"One and the same. Spent a lot of years tracking and fighting Comanche. Sorry to say it was our troop that recovered Quanah's mother, Cynthia Parker, and took her back to her family. Thought we was doing good. Woman died of a broken heart, they say . . . never accepted the birthing family. She'd turned wild, and her real family, except for the daughter that came with her, was out here on the plains living in tipis."

White Wolf suddenly felt very sleepy, and his eyelids fluttered as they struggled to stay open.

Goodnight evidently noticed. "Get some rest, Oliver. We need to get you eating, and I'll have some venison steaks and biscuits and coffee ready in a few hours."

40

TABITHA AND SHE Who Speaks had gone to the creek to bathe. Modesty was apparently not a part of the Comanche culture because this early morning many females of all ages and a few old men and small boys stood naked in the cool, clear water. She Who Speaks had already shrugged off her buckskin dress and, unencumbered by undergarments, stepped into the water. Tabitha hesitated for only a few moments before she began to disrobe, peeling off her boots and stockings, and then her trousers and shirt and, finally, her underthings, before she picked her way a bit timidly toward the water.

As she walked, she noticed all eyes were upon her, and she supposed she was something of a curiosity, although her natural, lightly-bronzed skin was only a shade lighter than that of some of the Comanche women. It occurred to her that a fair number of those, including the famous war chief, Quanah, were not pure bloods, and that the Comanche people's skins came in many hues of brownness. Several, presumably women who were originally brought to the band as captive children, had near ivory skin inside the tan lines left by their garments. She could not help but notice that She Who Speaks was not nearly as dark-skinned as her tanned face and arms might suggest. That, of course, would explain her proficiency in the English language. She would not have been an infant captive in that event.

After four days in the Comanche village, she knew little about She Who Speaks, and the woman was a formidable challenge to a reporter's inquisitive mind. Most of Tabitha's questions were met with stony silence. After the first day, her hostess's conversation had been limited to terse instructions. She was not cruel but was decidedly distant. Tabitha finally concluded she was to speak only when spoken to, so she switched to her powers of observation, making brief notes that would have been understood by no other person on the paper that had surprisingly been salvaged for her. She was baffled by why she had been accorded that privilege, but she was not going to 'look a gift horse in the mouth,' as her father always said.

Within limits she had been allowed to move about the village, and yesterday she had caught a glimpse of the three buffalo soldiers huddled together on the ground in a corner of the camp. It did not appear that further harm had come to them, and she was grateful for that.

Tabitha stepped upon the rocky creek bank, her feet tender to the sharp shards of stone. The bath had energized her and she found the thought of pulling on her filthy clothes, which she had worn for better than a week now, revolted her. She decided to abandon the under garments until she was given the opportunity to wash them. She wondered what kind of a wardrobe Comanche women maintained and if She Who Speaks would be amenable to sharing. She decided at that moment she would focus on acquiring the skills required for day-to-day Comanche life, even if she had to kill a buffalo and eat the liver raw, as Cal had once told her Comanche hunters did.

The prairie air had dried her flesh by the time she returned to her pile of clothing, where she encountered a naked Kwahadi woman holding up her cut-off cotton knickers and examining them with curiosity. She was quite young and pretty, although rather thick-set, and she looked at Tabitha and smiled. Tabitha smiled back and plucked her chemise from the pile and displayed it to her first friend. She slipped it over her head and pulled it down to her hips and twirled. Her friend laughed, and Tabitha pulled the garment off and handed it to the young woman. She pointed to the knickers and the chemise, touched her chest, and extended her hand, hoping she would understand Tabitha was making a gift. She obviously got the message because she beamed with obvious joy before scampering away. Tabitha turned and her eyes met those of She Who Speaks, who had evidently been watching the exchange. She nodded approvingly with faint traces of a smile on her lips.

After they returned to the tipi, Tabitha asked if she might gather some wood for the cooking fire. She Who Speaks studied her with apparent suspicion for several moments before nodding assent. While combing the banks of the creek for dead branches she saw Flying Crow and a half dozen small Comanche boys chasing a rabbit with their makeshift spears and lances. It appeared the rabbit would win this chase, but it brought to mind White Wolf's aborted rescue. She knew the army scout had been injured by the boy's attack, and she hoped it had not been seriously. She was confident that he had not been captured, as she would likely know about this. His death was another matter. It saddened her that his act of courage had been wasted, and it pained her that she had not been able to explain her reasons for remaining, but most certainly her chances of meeting death during the escape were greater than her remaining put. But it would make no sense to White Wolf.

She still marveled at Flying Crow's instinctive and vicious attack on the intruder in their tipi. Were all Comanche boys such young warriors? She would like to learn about this and these people. In her brief stay, to her surprise, she had found that The People were not the animals some whites claimed them to be. They loved and hated. They could be cruel and kind. They worked constantly at carrying out the tasks of daily life and survival. But they were human, just people set in a different culture. The thought had been nagging at her that she would like to tell their story, especially the tale of their last days as the rulers of the plains.

Watching the boys, as she moved upstream, she caught a glimpse of Flying Crow again, racing her way at the front of the pack, the rusty tint of his hair gleaming like copper in the sun. That's when it struck her. Something about the boy, besides his hostility, had been nagging at her. How could she have been so blind? His green-flecked brown eyes. The hair bleached lighter by the summer sun, but distinctively rusty at its roots. At that moment she was certain she was watching her nephew, Michael Levi Rivers, at play. The realization took her breath away, and she stopped and let herself down on a slab of protruding limestone to sit and collect her wits for a moment. Her new knowledge had to be dealt with carefully. She had a hunch her life could depend upon it.

She returned to their tipi with an armload of scrub wood and put it down next to the little fire pit outside. She ducked into the tipi and found She Who Speaks sitting off to one side, seemingly absorbed in serious thought, not even acknowledging Tabitha's appearance. Tabitha decided it was best to leave and give the woman her privacy and started to quietly back out of the tipi opening.

"Wait," She Who Speaks said, her voice barely above a whisper. "It is time for us to talk."

"I would like that," Tabitha replied, reversing her course and moving into the tipi and clearing a spot for herself on a buffalo robe. As she sat down, she noticed a small, folded pile of deerskin garments with a pair of moccasins on top within arm's reach.

"Those are for you. The moccasins are a gift from Doe Watcher. The other items were mine. They are yours now. They are well-worn but will serve their purpose, and I would guess they should fit adequately. You will seem much less a freak to the band if you abandon your own clothes for the time being."

"Thank you. But, Doe Watcher, who is she? Why would she give me the moccasins?" She took the moccasins from the stack and ran the tips of her fingers over them. "They are beautiful and so soft."

"Doe Watcher is the proud recipient of you dirty under garments. She brought the moccasins to the tipi in appreciation. She is known for her fine work with skins of all kinds, but moccasins are her specialty, I guess you would call it. She makes moccasins for many in the band in exchange for meat and hides and other necessities. Her husband is lazy and has not even taken a second wife because she supports him so well."

"I will have to find her and thank her."

"She will be easy enough to find. She passes through the village wearing nothing but your gifts, stretched to their limits, I fear."

Tabitha smiled at the image that formed in her mind. "I'm glad they please her."

"They do, but now to more serious business. Some decisions must be made about your future."

"I don't think I'm in a position to make a decision. The Comanche are making my decisions for me."

"That is true to a point. You are not free to leave. You may choose to die if you insist upon leaving, or you may choose to live as you are now if I tell Quanah you are remaining as my woman, so to speak."

"And, of course, there are conditions."

"Yes. You will not try to escape. And you will not agree to ransom. You will stay with the Comanche until the wars are over and the Kwahadi agree to go to the reservation."

"That might be years."

"Possibly, but not likely. Some of the chiefs have illusions they are fighting for a way of life. Quanah and a few others believe they are fighting for more favorable peace terms. He has told only a few, but he sees the end coming within a year."

"How do you know I will keep my word?"

"If someone negotiates your ransom, you will not leave the village alive. I have explained to Quanah this work you do as a reporter. I have also advised him it is not in the interest of the Kwahadi to have you writing stories about anything you have learned during your time here, including what I just told you."

"What if I told you I want to stay?"

"I would find this a very strange statement."

"I am a writer. I am curious. I want to learn about your people . . . and about you. And then I want to write about what I have learned and experienced. There will be stories for my newspaper and, possibly, a book. I will report what I see honestly and fairly. You could help me with this work and bring a unique perspective. You are not a blood Comanche, I'm sure of it . . . and neither is your son." She knew she was taking a risk in adding the last, but if she was going to travel a road with this woman she must start with truth.

There was a prolonged silence. She Who Speaks's eyes locked on Tabitha's as if trying to make up her mind about something. "We must have truth between us."

"Yes. And if we do we can help each other . . . and your people."

"I know your brother."

That was the last thing Tabitha expected to hear. My God, what next? "I have four brothers. Which one?" Somehow, she knew the answer that was coming.

"Joshua. He was briefly a captive at Palo Duro, along with a very beautiful and equally feisty woman."

"That would be Jessica Chandler."

"Yes, Jessica, that was what he called her."

"I knew they had been captured during Erin's ransoming, but he never said anything about meeting you."

"There would have been no reason. Our business was entirely legal. I act as Quanah's interpreter and sometime intermediary. Your brother is, in a sense, Quanah's lawyer. He was retained to ease the way to favorable peace terms. I last saw him several months ago after he was shot by some men who were following him, apparently with the objective of killing him for some reason."

"He never explained why he was out on the Staked Plains by

himself or who shot him. I just can't believe this. That is, I know you are telling me the truth. It is all more than I can comprehend at this moment. Another question then?"

"Of course."

"Josh doesn't know that your son is also his son, does he?"

This time, Tabitha saw that she had set off the dynamite. She Who Speaks averted her gaze and was visibly shaken. The hand that brushed back her hair was trembling noticeably.

"You're not making sense."

"I'm making perfect sense. Josh's infant son was taken captive by Comanche. Michael would have been about Flying Crow's age. I take that back. He is exactly Flying Crow's age to the second of birth. Because Michael and Flying Crow are one and the same person. And obviously Josh doesn't have a clue."

She Who Speaks seemed to regain her composure. "There is to be truth between us. First, Josh does not know. He has never seen my son. I suspected when I first saw Josh after his capture and learned he was seeking a captive boy about Flying Crow's age. I made certain Josh would not come across him in the village. I was still not certain at that time. But at our meeting after Josh was wounded, I spent more time with him and studied his features . . . especially the eyes, only slightly less so, the rust-colored hair. But the eyes are very unusual."

"Michael had a nasty scar on his left arm. I hadn't given it a thought before I realized the truth, but Flying Crow has a scar at the same spot. This is too much for coincidence. I'm sharing a tipi with my lost nephew, and he doesn't even like me."

"It's not that. You are one of the white eyes he has been raised to hate. As you become one of us in dress and habit, he will be less hostile. Also, to this point, he has received no signals from me as to how he should react. That will change. And he will change."

"Does he speak any English? I have only heard him speak Comanche, but sometimes I have the feeling he understands what we are saying."

She Who Speaks smiled. "His English is excellent, but I have not been able to teach him to read and write. Perhaps, you can help with that, and he can teach you some Comanche."

"Sooner or later, we are going to meet up with Josh again. What happens then?"

"He will not take my son. Ever. That much you must accept if we are to be friends."

41

DANNA SINCLAIR AND Marty Locke sat in the Rivers and Sinclair conference room. The room's designation at some past time had been tongue in cheek because it was about the size of a large closet with a table four feet in length and a bit over two feet in width. Four captain's chairs pressed against the walls barely allowed room for the occupants to squeeze in. One of the narrow walls, however, consisted mostly of a window that afforded ample light and some occasional air.

"Why is this called a conference room?" Marty asked.

Danna shrugged. "I asked Josh that one time, and he just said every law office has to have a conference room. This is ours."

"Well, being on the west side of the building, it is cooler in the morning, and we've got a nice breeze coming in the window right now."

Danna was impatient with small talk. "Have you learned any more about George Hatter and Judge Robinson?"

"No. Except George is still making his visits to the judge's office. Have you noticed that George is on the nervous side lately, sort of like a hen at a mass meeting of coyotes?"

"Are we the coyotes?"

"Could be."

"I'd sure like to confront him before I boot him out on his fat ass. We know he leaked our involvement with Quanah, and he's tipped somebody off about Josh's travels. But we can't prove a damn thing."

"Keep your enemies close. Now that we know the man's not to be trusted, we just have to bypass him with anything important. He can still write a decent land contract and earn his pay. We'll figure this out soon."

There was a soft tapping on the door before Linda opened it. She gently nudged a little Mexican boy in front of her. "This young gentleman has a message for Mr. Locke. He said Mr. Locke will pay him only if he delivers it personally."

Marty fished a coin from his pocket and handed it to the boy, and the little courier produced an envelope and gave it to the lawyer. "Gracias, señor," he said, and turned and scurried down the hallway. Linda de la Cruz closed the door and followed.

Danna lifted her brow questioningly as Marty worked the envelope open and removed the note, which seemed to be written on a little piece of scratch paper. He read it aloud. "You want to take me to lunch this noon. The Exchange. T." He shrugged. "It's from Tara."

"And?"

"She can be surprisingly blunt but generally not without purpose."

"Then I gather you had better be prepared to buy her lunch. I suspect you would not find that an undue burden."

He grinned sheepishly. "Not too undue."

42

Tara Cahill was already seated at a small table next to a wall in The Exchange dining room when Marty walked through the wide entryway. She signaled with a quick discrete wave, and he joined her at the table. As he sat down, Tara said, "I've ordered ham and sourdough bread sandwiches for both of us . . . with coffee and cherry pie. Ham isn't always available here, and it seemed like a nice change. I hope that's alright. You can afford this, can't you?"

He found her mischievous smile charming, but he had enjoyed her company on several evenings since the first time, and it occurred to him he was starting to find everything about this young woman charming. He found himself making excuses to walk his own documents to the court for filing these days, and after every encounter he looked for excuses for another. He wasn't certain how she felt, though. She was very coy and kept him guessing. "I can afford lunch," he said, "and although I truly enjoy your company, I have some hope that you had an interesting reason for inviting yourself to dine with me."

The young Mexican waiter delivered their sandwiches and

coffee with a promise he would return later with the pie. She waited until he was beyond hearing range before she spoke. "I'll let you be the judge of that. I've written nothing down. I hope you are an attentive listener and have a decent memory."

"Try me."

"Well, there is nothing in my story that makes me look more virtuous than a cheap spy who sells information for free meals. I may be deluding myself that I am serving a noble cause. I guess that remains to be seen. Are you a servant of noble causes?"

"If they pay well enough."

"Please say something to make me feel better about all of this."

"You may be saving a man's life. You could expedite peace with the Comanche."

"There now, I knew you could do it. I feel so much better."

"Perhaps you should tell me what you have learned. The lunch hour clock is running."

"Judge Robinson has been out of the office for a week and won't return for a few days, and my fellow office workers know I've been working though the noon hour for three days running . . . while the office was closed. They won't grumble if I'm a few minutes late."

"Please, Tara, don't torment me like this."

She reached across the table and softly patted his hand, and his heart took a leap. "But it's so much fun," she said with an impish smile. "Very well. I've searched the judge's office and found some interesting letters and papers. Organized man that he is, he had a nice history of certain activities filed away in a locked desk drawer."

"How did you get in?"

"With a key."

"How did you find it?"

"He had a single pottery vase on his fireplace mantel. That's probably where you'd put a key isn't it?"

He shrugged. "I might." Truth was, he probably would.

"Men think they're so clever, but they can be so simple-minded. Anyway, I opened the desk drawer and made myself at home. In a matter of minutes I found dozens of notes from a man named Hilton Seymour, who apparently represents someone who was always referred to as 'SW.'"

"Simon Willard. He's in charge of contracts for everything needed by the military . . . food supplies, horses, equipment, and just about anything you can think of."

"Judge Robinson and a man referred to as 'Hidalgo' are apparently major providers of merchandise for the military. The drawer was stuffed with procurement orders of one kind or another, mostly for horses and cattle, but sometimes flour and other foodstuffs. One interesting note from Seymour stated that 'ten percent was not enough and that the new rate was fifteen, returned at the time of payment.' Is this what it appears to be?"

"Sounds like 'SW' gets a kickback in exchange for the contracts with the judge and his future father-in-law."

"There were some other notes. One told the judge to have 'Hatter' report whenever Rivers was leaving town and to find out where he was headed. Another said that Rivers was trying to negotiate a settlement that would put the Comanche in the horse and cattle business. 'Not good. Even worse than end of wars,' the note added."

"Tara, you struck gold. This answers a lot of questions, and it just might save some lives . . . lots of them. I'll explain another time. Anything else I should know."

"I think I've given you a pretty good summary of what I found." A glum look settled on her face. "I'll be quitting my job when the judge returns, so I may have to head back East."

"Why?"

"Now that I know what I do about the judge's dealings, I can't continue to work for him. Besides, I've been dishonest in my own way in searching into his private papers. No matter the purpose, I feel like a criminal."

Marty felt genuinely contrite. First, he led the young woman into her detective work. And he did not want her leaving Santa Fe. It would not be the same without her.

"You did the right thing," he said. "I promise. We'll talk about this again in a few days. Everything will work out for you. I guarantee it." But, of course, he couldn't.

43

"THE SON-OF-a-bitch," Danna hissed, after Marty had relayed his conversation with Tara Cahill. "Hatter's out of this office before the day is out."

They were sitting in Danna's private office. She had already satisfied herself that George Hatter was passing information to Judge Robinson. Obviously, Hatter's motive was money. But she had been unable to figure out why anybody would be paying the law clerk for information. Now she understood.

"Danna, there's something else I'd like to throw out for consideration . . . only indirectly related to this."

"Yes."

"Tara Cahill. She's going to be leaving the court office. We're going to have a vacancy here. What would you think about her filling George's spot in our office? She has the background for it."

Danna studied Marty's face, but, as usual, it didn't reveal much. "You have more than a casual interest in this lady, don't you?"

"Yes. I like her. She's smart as a whip, and I won't deny I find her attractive. But our relationship is barely teetering on the brink of friendship right now."

"Sometimes romantic interests among employees in a business enterprise can wreak havoc."

"I'm aware of that, but I'm not a kid, and this young woman is mature beyond her years. I'm confident we can deal with working together no matter where our private lives take us."

Danna considered his remarks. Marty was perhaps a half dozen years older than herself, had been a military officer, and started and lost a family. He was certain she and Josh would offer him a partnership in the firm within a year. He was entitled to make a suggestion and have it respected. And the firm owed plenty to Tara Cahill. Josh wasn't available to consult, and, as managing partner, Danna was entitled to make the decision. "Tell her to stop by and see me as soon as her job at the court is finished. I've met her at the clerk's office and she seems efficient and businesslike, but I need to speak with her."

"I appreciate this."

"Now, we need to get the nasty business with George Hatter taken care of."

"Do you want to meet with him privately?"

"I'd like you to sit in on the meeting. And feel free to join the conversation, if you wish, but it's my job to do the deed."

Marty stood up. "I'll call him in, but I'll let you do the talking."

When Marty returned with George Hatter, it was apparent the man knew he was showing up for an execution. His face was white as fresh snow. She supposed he was too smart not to have picked up on the changes in the office routine lately. They had been bypassing Hatter with important projects and the contacts with him had turned ice cold. Small talk within the office had evaporated. Even the usually ebullient Linda, although not informed of what was taking place, had turned quiet and tentative, obviously aware something was not right in the house of Rivers and Sinclair.

"George, be seated," Danna said, "we're going to have a chat."

Hatter obeyed, casting a wary glance at Marty, who was moving a chair off to one side of Danna's desk, leaving Hatter alone in front of it. There was a prolonged silence, during which Danna studied the accused's face, watching the beads of perspiration starting to erupt.

Finally, she spoke. "George, are you acquainted with Simon Willard, the General Procurement Officer for the armies of the Southwest?"

The man's eyes widened. "No, ma'am. I know who he is, but I'm not personally acquainted."

"What about his assistant, Hilton Seymour?" She was surprised not to see the man's britches darken with piss.

"I've met him a time or two. But I barely know him."

"Where did you meet him?"

"I . . . I don't remember. At a tavern maybe."

"But you're a teetotaler, George, and I've never known you to frequent taverns."

Evidently shoring up his courage, he snapped back. "I said I didn't remember. I hardly know the man."

She decided to hit him directly. "Why have you been leaking information from our office, George, especially about Josh's travels?"

Hatter huffed up like an angry rooster. "Who says I've been doing that? They're a damned liar." While he had turned feisty, perspiration was now streaming down his face.

"What are your visits to Judge Robinson's office about?"

"What in the hell are you talking about? I'm not visiting the Judge's office. I make court filings with his clerks. That's all I do."

"You're lying through your teeth, George. Marty has followed you there, and we have other witnesses. Now, why in the hell would a judge be having frequent meetings with a law clerk? You're not admitted to the bar. You can't even handle simple motions in chambers."

"The judge is a friend. We talk about things."

"Like kickbacks from government supply contracts? Killing Josh to keep him from negotiating peace with the Comanche? Here's what I think. You are being paid for reporting confidential client information from this office to the judge who, in turn, passes it along to Seymour, who either acts on it or sends it on to his boss, Willard. You may be the low man on the totem pole, but you are a part of a conspiracy to steal from the United States government, and you are potentially an accessory to attempted murder." She stood up. "Now, Marty's going to watch while you collect your personal things. Anything you can't clear out in fifteen minutes stays. Don't ever come within twenty feet of this office again. If you're as smart as you think you are, you will get out of Santa Fe before the scandal breaks."

Hatter rose from his chair and was out of the door in a flash. Marty followed.

Danna sat back down and tried to sort out the legal implications of what they knew about the judge and his accomplices. In less than ten minutes, Marty returned.

"He can move fast when he has to," Danna observed, as Marty reclaimed his chair and turned it toward her.

"I'm guessing that after he fills in the judge, he'll be leaving for other parts. What do you think comes of this?"

"I don't think there will be any more efforts on Josh's life from that source. We are, of course, going to have a very uneasy relationship with Robinson in the future. I don't think we have enough solid evidence to go over his head at this point. Tara's testimony is somewhat tainted, and even taken at face value, it is very difficult to put together all of the links in the chain. We're still left with a lot of speculation and circumstantial evidence. I suppose my disclosures to George Hatter will result in a lot of evidence being destroyed, but I felt I had to let them know that we were on to them in order to get them to back off."

"There will be other opportunities. People like that don't get religion overnight. Now I think I need to get back to some paying business."

44

OLIVER WOLF, AS he had been anointed by Charlie Goodnight, had fully recovered from his wound. Once the pus had drained, the flesh had started to heal quickly. Close to two weeks had passed since the aborted rescue, and the last four days Wolf had been helping Goodnight scout the Palo Duro Canyon floor. He sat astride Storm on the rim near the southern outlet. The panoramic view of the canyon from above was breathtaking, and as they had begun exploring the nooks and crannies below, it was no less impressive. A healthy flow of water from a narrow river that snaked its way through the canyon's bottom was nourished even further by springs along its journey. He had seen more lush grass in Arkansas and further east but not in Texas. He was not a cattleman—although Goodnight had him learning—but common sense told him the man had it figured right. Cattle would thrive in this country.

He watched as Goodnight walked his chestnut-colored mare up the tricky, deer trail that wound around sharp turns as it worked up the crumbling canyon wall. It was a tension-filled trek that he had completed himself a short time ago.

While he waited for Goodnight to join him, his eyes picked up a cloud of dust crawling along the flatter lands beyond the southern exit of the canyon. The plume was too small for buffalo, too large for deer. He concluded the dust was being raised by three or four horses, and based upon the numbers, they were likely mounted. They were headed due east in the direction of the Kwahadi village. Comanche? Or fools headed for the mouth of hell? They presented no threat to him and Goodnight, but Wolf found himself curious as hell.

When Goodnight led his horse over the canyon rim, Wolf pointed toward the dust cloud. Goodnight steadied the mare and unfastened his saddlebag and pulled out his mariner's telescope. He spent a few moments wiping off the lens and fiddling with some of the knobs before he pressed it to his eye, mumbling to himself as he tried to focus. Wolf had noticed Goodnight was given to one-man conversations. Too much time alone? "Two riders with pack animals. Not Comanche. Do we want to meet them?"

"They're heading in the direction of the Comanche village. Of course, it might be on purpose. And they would have a good three or four days' ride in front of them. They might veer away long before they're in danger."

"Oh, what the hell, curiosity's got the best of me. We can catch up in a few hours. I know a short cut. Let's go see who else is crazy enough to be wandering around this godforsaken country without military escort."

A few hours later they had nearly reached the strangers, moving in on them from their north side. He knew they had been spotted when the riders reined in their horses and turned toward them, waiting and watching cautiously but with no sign of hostility as he and Goodnight approached.

They were both relatively young men, probably short of thirty, Wolf guessed. They showed the wear of a long ride, dust-coated and wind-burned faces—tired eyes. Both were tall and rangy men, he could tell by the way they sat in their saddles. The man whose hair and beard were the color of wheat straw was probably an inch or two short of six and a half feet. Wolf couldn't explain it, but it seemed he was the rougher cut of the two and appeared to fit in more on the plains. The man with reddish hair was no dandy, but his buckskin gelding carried an expensive saddle, and the rider's dirty shirt and trousers suggested high quality even to Wolf's uneducated eye.

As they drew closer, Goodnight spoke first. "Gentlemen, we come peaceably. Saw you from upon the canyon rim to the north and got to admit we was curious about you and thought we ought to warn you there's a hornet's nest in the direction you're headed."

The man with rusty-looking hair dismounted. "Get down and we'll talk a spell."

Wolf and Goodnight followed his cue, and after casting his eyes studiously in all directions, the blond, shaggy-haired rider joined them.

"I'm Josh Rivers. This is my brother, Cal." He extended his hand and Wolf accepted the firm grip, and Goodnight followed, and Calvin Rivers stepped forward to offer his.

Goodnight said, "I'm Charlie Goodnight, and this here's my friend, Oliver Wolf."

It seemed strange to Wolf to hear his recently awarded name spoken in full, but he didn't correct it. But stranger yet was the last name of the strangers, and he was sure he had heard their names spoken before.

Josh Rivers said, "You mentioned we were headed toward a hornet's nest. Care to explain?"

"I'll let Oliver tell you about it."

The men looked expectantly at Wolf who decided to start at the end of the story, but thought he would first toss a little surprise to the visitors and hook their attention. "Josh, I understand you are a lawyer, and, Cal, I believe you are currently in the ranching business and that you were once an army scout like myself."

Both men stared at him incredulously.

Josh said, "Should I know you from someplace?"

"No, but I know your sister very well. I last saw her in the camp of a Kwahadi band."

"She's alive then?"

"She was at that time, very much so. And knowing her as I do, I'm very confident she's still alive. She seemed to be well on the way to surviving when I made a fool of myself." He then proceeded to tell the story of Tabitha's capture and his foiled attempt to rescue her from the Comanche village. "If I hadn't come across Goodnight here, I wouldn't be telling this story."

"We are on our way to ransom Tabby or get her out of that Comanche village one way or the other," Josh said.

Goodnight said. "Texas covers a lot of country. I'm curious how you happened to be down this way. Damn big coincidence we'd meet up like this."

"Not so big," Cal said. "I was an army scout with Mackenzie. I've covered this country again and again. It's not that hard to figure out about where Quanah's going to be. Actually, he's running out of places to hide out. He'll be moving out this way soon. He can't resist stopping at the canyon. If we just settled in here, he'd show up sooner or later."

"But we're not waiting," Josh interjected.

Goodnight said, "I've been scouting Palo Duro Canyon for ranching prospects. Sounds like it's about time for me to finish up and head out."

"Mr. Wolf," Josh said, "you told us you watched the activity in the village and saw my sister walking with a woman there. Did she appear to be talking with this woman?"

Wolf pondered the question, putting together the pieces of that afternoon and evening. "She was. Definitely. They were speaking with each other. Not in a chatty way, but there words exchanged between them. I didn't give it a thought at the time, but now that I think about it, this was very strange."

"What did this woman look like?" Josh asked.

"Quite slender. About Tabitha's size, now that I consider it. I wasn't near enough to make out her features."

"She Who Speaks, also known a Jael Chernik."

"You know this woman?"

"I've met her. She was a captive, adopted into the band. She has learned multiple languages and made herself useful to Quanah in particular as an interpreter. She has some influence as a counselor."

Wolf responded. "Perhaps that's why Tabitha was determined to stay behind. She may be under the protection of this woman, but that is fragile. In the end the Comanche will do what they want."

"Well," Josh said, "Cal and I are on our way to get Tabitha out of there before they change their minds."

"Let me go with you," Wolf said. "I know exactly where the

village is if they haven't packed up and moved. Regardless, we should be able to track that many people from the site without any trouble."

"I appreciate the offer," Josh said, "but we intend to ride right into the village. If somebody recognizes you as the man who tried the rescue a few weeks back, it might not go so well for any of us."

"I understand, but I would like to do something."

"You tried. Sometimes that's all we can do. Besides, it seems to me the army's going to be wondering what became of you. Don't you think it's time to report back?"

"Yes, I'd better, but I sure hate to go back with my tail between my legs."

Cal observed, "You're damned lucky you're going back with your balls between your legs." Then he turned to Goodnight. "Are you the fella that rode with the Texas Rangers?"

45

TABITHA LAY NAKED on a soft buffalo robe in the tipi she shared with her Comanche hostess and her son, the feisty boy who was also Tabitha's nephew. The night, after a blistering daytime heat, had not brought much relief from the stifling heat, and the little breeze that sifted through the air openings was too feeble to ward off the oven-like blast. Clothes stuck to one's skin like they were pasted in this situation, and along with her roommates, she had quickly learned to shuck both her clothes and her modesty.

She surmised from their rhythmic breathing on the other side of the tipi that her roommates were sleeping soundly. Tabitha could not join their slumber because of the steady drumbeats and chanting coming from the far end of the camp. Jael had seemed in a hurry to rush her off to their robes tonight, with a rather brusque explanation that the men were gathering for a ceremonial evening. But she definitely heard women's voices among the chanters and singers.

She was finding herself becoming quite comfortable in the Comanche encampment. On the other hand, she knew she was nothing if not adaptable. It had been a week now since she had been brought as a captive to the camp, and she felt she and Jael were laying the foundations for trust between them, and they had certainly formed an alliance that was moving toward friendship. It was Jael who had suggested that between the two of them her former name be used, especially since the Comanche pronunciation of her name was almost impossible for the white tongue to enunciate, and the English version was a bit cumbersome for conversation.

Suddenly, a horrifying scream echoed through the darkness. And then another. And another. The chanting grew louder and louder, and the drumbeats came faster, but they did not drown out the incessant screaming. Tabitha sat up and snatched up her dress and moccasins and crept out the tipi opening. Outside, she pulled the doeskin dress over her head and slipped into her moccasins. Then, slowly and quietly, she wove her way through the maze of tipis led by the ear-shattering screams that rose above the other eerie voices and drumming that never seemed to quit. She stopped abruptly just outside the range of the orange glow of the fire. She edged behind some drying deerskins that were stretched out on poles near one of the tipis. From here she had a fairly clear view of the celebration.

When her eyes fastened on the objects in the center of the mass of chanting Comanche, she turned away and wretched and vomited. Staked out naked on the ground not far from the spitting fire were two of the buffalo soldiers. One had a smoldering coal planted in each eye, and his stomach had been sliced from groin to sternum, and his guts had spilled from his abdomen. A gaping, bloody hole was all that remained of his penis and scrotum. He had obviously been scalped, because his kinky-haired scalp was split by a wide strip of raw, bleeding meat.

He was no longer screaming, and she assumed he was either unconscious or dead. She hoped he was dead.

The other soldier was not so fortunate. His screams had subsided, but his sobs had not. She saw a slightly-built warrior circling him and realized it was Sour Face, the warrior who had tried to rape her. She had since learned that his name was Hawk Talons. Tonight he paraded around the council fire like a circus ringmaster announcing acts, she thought. The black man who lay spread-eagled near the fire still had his eyes and sight, but they just allowed him to watch the red-hot fire coals that had been piled on his stomach, as they burned their way through his tender flesh. She watched in horror as Sour Face made a sudden turn and stepped between the victim's legs, bent over and began sawing on the man's scrotum with a stone knife. After mere moments, Sour Face raised his hand, clutching the dark, blood-slick sack that contained the man's balls. A squaw broke into the fire circle, fingers outreached, and Sour Face tossed her the trophy.

Suddenly, a hand clasped over her mouth, and a strong arm wrapped about Tabitha's waste and yanked her backward. She was pulled behind a tipi, and a voice whispered in her ear. "Quiet. Not a word. I'm going to release you."

She turned and faced Jael, whose lips were sealed tight and whose eyes shot spears of anger. Jael grabbed her arm roughly and began dragging her away from the fire and did not release her iron grip until they returned to their tipi. Then she pushed Tabitha toward her buffalo robe. "Don't say a word. You risk your life if you leave again. We will talk tomorrow."

Tabitha disrobed and lay back down on her sleeping place, but she did not sleep that night. She could not release the nightmare from her mind, and her thoughts turned to Zeke. The massive buffalo soldier had not been staked out on the ground tonight. Was there hope for him yet? It was strange, she thought, she barely knew the other two soldiers and she was deeply aggrieved about the end they met. Still, it was always more profound when someone near and dear was involved. We hear of atrocities around the world, and they may sadden us, but we shrug them off. Too bad such things happen to people. The death of a stranger is a passing thought, a tragedy only to those who loved or cared for him. It becomes a truly sorrowful event only if it is our own family member or a dear friend who has suffered or died. She still tried to deny what she had witnessed. And the thought of Zeke enduring the same torment nearly drove her mad.

The next morning Tabitha was not brave enough to broach the subject of the previous night's events with Jael. She went about her camp chores and, for the second day, worked with Flying Crow on his alphabet, showing him how all of the confusing letters could spell his name. He seemed annoyed that he had to put up with the lessons, yet he obviously could not resist the challenge. His initial hostility seemed to have faded away, and he had at least accepted that she was going to be sharing their tipi for the foreseeable future. He was a bright boy, and she found herself enjoying these moments when she could toss a surprise word out for his vocabulary.

After the boy was dismissed to join his friends, Jael returned to the tipi. "Come with me," she said. "We are going to take a walk."

Tabitha got up and followed.

"You were very foolish when you left our tipi last night," Jael scolded, as they walked down the slope toward the creek. "I did not want you to see what was happening."

"I gathered as much. I heard the screams, and my curiosity got the best of me. And I will never forget what I saw. It was barbaric and sickening. I cannot believe people can take such joy in the torture and maiming of other people." She shook her head. "Those poor men . . . to die such a terrible death."

"This is what The People do to their enemies, and it is what their traditional enemies would do to them if circumstances were reversed."

"But our soldiers do not torture. It is not a part of our culture."

"They do terrible things. They attack undefended villages and rape and kill the women and girls. They bash in the heads of babies with the butts of their rifles or behead them with their long knives. No child is spared when they attack. Twice I have escaped such slaughter with Flying Crow, but I saw with my own eyes the work of your own savages. Do not lecture me on the moral differences of our people."

Tabitha realized she was not going to win this war of words. Someday she would write of what she witnessed, and she would learn more of the Comanche viewpoint and report the atrocities committed by her own people. For now, she had more immediate concerns. "What about Sergeant Hooper? They have not harmed him, have they?"

They strolled along the creek bank while Jael seemed to be pondering the question. Jael stopped and removed her moccasins and sat down on the creek bank and dangled her feet in swift-flowing cool water. Tabitha joined her.

"Sergeant Hooper, as you call him, is seen as a great warrior.

He is a physical giant and has refused to exhibit fear. Among the Kwahadi it is an honor for him to face his death alone."

"Then he will be tortured."

"When the circle of the moon is filled, about a week from now. There will be a great celebration."

"I want to save him. I had hoped the others would not be harmed. We spoke to Quanah, and he said he would try."

"He did try. You must understand that Quanah is a war chief, but our band has other chiefs, as well, who have different views. One of these is Isa-tai, who is also a shaman, who wields great influence with the council."

"I have seen him. He is a squat, little man with bulging eyes."

"Yes, he looks like a toad doesn't he?" They both giggled.

"He doesn't look like a man of influence."

"I am struggling for the words, but there is a saying for that."

"Looks can be deceiving?"

"Yes, that's it. But my point is that there are a half dozen or more in the band who have rank and influence in these matters. Quanah and Isa-tai are both young men, and while Quanah is respected for his skills at war-making, the older chiefs often listen to Isa-tai because he tells them what they want to hear."

"I guess whites and Comanche are not all that different in that respect."

"We will meet with Quanah again, perhaps with the entire council, about the fate of the buffalo soldier, but I have something else to discuss."

"Yes?"

"Your brother, the lawyer, is traveling this way. Our scouts report he is accompanied by a tall, yellow-haired man who was seen with One Hand Mackenzie during the battles of a year ago.

I may have seen this man when the red-haired woman was ransomed."

"If you were involved in the ransom exchange, you may have seen him. When I last spoke with him, he was planning to marry the red-haired woman. The man would be my brother, Cal."

"It is believed the riders are seeking our village, and they seem to be on a direct course. For some reason, they appear to know exactly where to find us. That is worrisome to Quanah. We will likely be moving very soon, but Quanah and the other members of the council will wait until they hear what your brother has to say. They are probably two days' ride from here. You and I must have an understanding. The lives of both of your brothers depend upon it."

"Go on."

"Your brother is expected to be coming to conduct business with Quanah. I doubt if he knows of your presence here, and certainly he has no reason to know Flying Crow is his son. You and Flying Crow must remain in the tipi while your brothers are in the village. We do not want them to know that either of you are here."

"But I have told you I want to stay."

"And if he is aware of your presence, you will have the opportunity to tell him that. You must not say a word about Flying Crow, however. You must understand that if your brother learns of Flying Crow's presence and that if he attempts to take him, he will die before he leaves the village with my son. I will kill him myself, if necessary, to stop him. Every warrior in the village will rise to support me. Many would like the excuse to kill two white men, especially to give them the death that was delivered to the buffalo soldiers last night. Remember, Flying

Crow is Comanche, and white men are not allowed to abduct our children."

46

THE CROWD WAS growing. Cal had first spotted the Comanche scouts yesterday, commenting that he had felt them before he saw them. At first there were two, but now there were a half dozen Indians split on each side about fifty yards out. It was a positive sign, Josh thought. There had been no harassment or feints in their direction, so Cal had suggested the Comanche riders made up more of an escort than anything else.

An hour and five more Comanche later, the village was in sight, and Josh caught sight of a delegation riding out in a cloud of dust to meet them. They reined in and waited. He had mixed feelings when he spotted She Who Speaks among the riders. He was surprised to find his heart raced a bit at the sight of her. She was indeed a woman who would catch the eye of most men, and he wished the circumstances were different.

On the other hand, he felt anger at her deception. He was almost certain this woman held Michael captive. When the time was right, he would find out. He wondered if she would lie about Tabby's capture as well. The Comanche riders pulled up twenty paces in front of them, and then She Who Speaks kneed her black mare forward.

"Josh, we were not expecting you. We had not sent a messenger."

"Greetings, She Who Speaks—or is it Jael now?"

"Jael is acceptable."

"Your messenger is dead. Killed apparently by someone who is in no hurry to see peace between the Kwahadi and the white soldiers."

"We will find another messenger. But you must have business. You would not have come this far to tell us that our courier had been killed."

"I have progress to report on the negotiations. And I have other very important business," he added meaningfully.

She did not flinch. "Then we will try to address all of your business. Now, follow us into the village. Quanah is waiting."

Surprisingly, Quanah sat alone in his tipi. After Josh and Cal were seated, Jael explained to Quanah Cal's relationship to Josh, and Cal received a solemn nod. Jael and Quanah spoke at some length in Comanche, and it seemed to Josh they were either arguing or debating something.

Finally, Jael turned to Josh and said, "Quanah says you have not chosen a good time to visit. Mackenzie is in the field, and we will be moving the camp early tomorrow morning. You will not be able to stay the night."

They obviously did not want Josh and Cal to linger. It was only mid-morning. They had deliberately camped not far from the village, thinking they might not be welcome to make an extended stay after Josh raised some unpleasant subjects. "We will try to take care of our business quickly and hope you will cooperate. I think I have made serious progress toward a peace settlement. I have met with Dr. Sturm who is very influential in these matters. He is arranging for me to meet with emissaries of President Grant in early fall."

Jael interpreted for Quanah who responded with questions. Jael said, "Quanah is impressed that the Great White Father is considering this matter but wishes to know what is attainable."

"We never know what is attainable for certain, but I am going to focus on three or four things. First, there should be no imprisonment for Quanah or any of the other chiefs. Second, there will be no signed treaty. The chiefs would simply lead your people to the reservation. I think this makes the Comanche side of the peace a matter of honor. The whites do not have a good record of keeping treaties."

Again Jael interpreted. Quanah smiled a bit, shaking his head in agreement, and replied in Comanche. Jael continued, "He appreciates your remark about the white man's keeping of treaties, and, of course, if prison is the fate of the chiefs they will fight to the death before being caged."

"I will also ask for land under the ownership and control of the tribe and cattle so you can raise your own meat. I would insist on a provision for a monthly stipend, but I need to meet with the President's representatives before I can determine amounts. My question is this: if I can obtain these commitments, will the Comanche come to the reservation?"

After a long dialogue with the chief, Jael said, "These are things that are very important to Quanah's thinking. He emphasizes he does not make the decision alone, but he is confident he can convince most of the chiefs of accepting terms near to these. He says you should work on the specific provisions, and he has other concerns about peace he wants to discuss. But when you bring a definite proposal from the Great White Father, it will be presented to the council, and he should be able to support it."

They talked for another hour about details of any peace terms, and Josh felt he understood what would be acceptable and what would not. He decided this subject had been exhausted, and he abruptly shifted to his next concern. "My sister and three buffalo soldiers are being held captives in this village, and I want to take them back with me. This would be an enormous showing of good faith and would help greatly in successful peace negotiations."

A long, awkward silence. Josh noticed that Jael, in contrast to her usual calm demeanor, was visibly shaken. Her eyes momentarily looked like those of a frightened doe, and she bit her lip nervously. She recovered after a few moments and began speaking to Quanah. He seemed to be protesting something, and the tone of her voice became insistent and near demanding. Quanah got up and left the tipi.

"Quanah must speak to some of the chiefs," she said. "You wait here." She also got up and started for the tipi opening, but Josh stopped her.

"I forgot to mention," he said. "I expect to take my son back with me."

She did not respond and kept on moving.

"Damn," Cal said, "you sure got a knack for stirring up trouble."

47

JAEL HAD RETURNED to Quanah's tipi and instructed Josh and Cal to follow her. She led them to another tipi, one that was noticeably smaller than that of the war chief. She entered, and they found Tabitha standing just inside the entryway. She moved to her brothers and hugged them each enthusiastically.

"Josh and Cal. It's a family reunion. I'm glad you're okay."

"Us? You're the one that's the prisoner."

"Me? No, I'm not. Well, I was, but not anymore."

"Then you'll be going with us."

Jael backed out of the tipi, and Josh felt more comfortable with her departure. The family had things to discuss.

"I won't be leaving with you, Josh," Tabitha announced.

"What do you mean? You said you're not a prisoner anymore."

"I'm not. I'm staying voluntarily. I want to write stories— maybe a book—about the final days of the Comanche wars. You can't get any more inside than this."

"Are you insane? Do you know how dangerous it is here? You never know when these people will turn on you, and our own army will be firing on Indians. Bullets don't discriminate between red and white when they're coming this way. I won't let you do this damn foolishness."

Cal intervened. "He's right, sis. This is going to be in the middle of hell when the army and Comanche finally have it out. Have you really thought about this?"

"I've done little else but think about it." She turned on Josh. "And you don't have a damn thing to say about it, big brother. You're not my guardian."

Josh sighed deeply. This was a hell of a development. They came to rescue a sister who refused to be rescued. "Now I know how Oliver felt."

"Who's Oliver?" she snapped.

"Oliver Wolf. He tried to get you out of here and about died for it."

"I don't know any Oliver Wolf. An army scout by the name of White Wolf tried to get me out of here. He must be your Oliver. Is he alright? I felt terrible about the situation, and I've worried myself sick about him."

"He's fine now," Cal said. "He made his way to a man who helped him."

"Thank God. He's a good man."

"Now," Josh said, "Back to this matter of your staying with the Comanche."

"It's been decided. I just want you to get Sergeant Hooper out of here. He's a dead man if you don't."

"What about the others?"

"Too late."

She seemed unwilling to explain. "We're trying to free the Sergeant. Quanah says the Kwahadi are getting ready to move.

That might help. They sure as hell won't want to drag along a prisoner. Of course, that could speed up his end, too. And then there's the matter of Michael."

"Jael said you know."

"Damn right I know. And I can't talk sense into your head, I guess. But I'm taking Michael home."

"This is home."

"What do you mean by that?"

"As far as he knows or remembers, this is home. Jael's his mother. You take him now, by force, and you become the captor. It pains me to say this, but I've been with him a month now, lived with him and Jael in the same tipi. His blood says he's Michael, but he's Comanche, and he knows no mother but Jael. Think about this, Josh. She won't let you and Cal out of here alive with him anyway. If you try this, I'll just have two brothers who died needlessly. You may think I'm a fool, but please don't be one yourself."

There was a rustling of a tent flap, and Jael entered, pushing an obviously angry little boy ahead of her. This hostile boy had shoulder-length, rust-colored hair and Josh's distinctive brown-green eyes. He glared at Josh defiantly.

Josh's body went nearly numb, and his stomach fluttered. His emotions jumped between grief for the lost years and joy for what he saw as the end of his quest. He moved toward the boy and knelt down, extending his arms to embrace the boy. "Michael," he said softly.

"Flying Crow," the boy nearly screamed, backing away a few steps.

"You speak English?"

"I am Comanche."

"No, you are my son. Michael. You are not Comanche."

The boy slipped a little stone knife from the leather strip that held up his breechclout and charged Josh, slashing madly with the weapon. It carved a single slash in Josh's cheek and gouged his forearm before Jael wrapped her arms around the boy and drug him back. She wrenched the knife from his hand and tossed it aside. She spoke harshly to the boy in Comanche before he calmed and seemed only partly contrite.

"Tabby and Cal, could you give the three of us some time?"

"Of course, come on Cal, I'll show you the sights."

"Let me look at those wounds, Josh," Jael said.

He sat back on one of the robes, as she dropped to her knees to examine the injuries. After looking at her son's handiwork, she went to the far side of the tipi and rummaged through some supplies before returning with a small bag and a wet animal skin, which she used to wipe the blood away from his wounds. Then she dipped her fingers into the bag and brought out a clump of something that to Josh had a lard-look to it. She deftly applied the ointment.

"Take this with you," she said. "It will help seal the wounds in addition to healing them. I'm sorry this happened." She nodded toward Michael-Flying Crow. "I fear he's not."

She sat down, facing him, no more than five feet away. "Now we must talk. First we shall speak of realities. Our son is not going with you. I would kill you first, and if I am unsuccessful, there are five warriors outside this tipi prepared to do so. Your brother would die and so would the buffalo soldier. If you leave without further incident, three of you may have safe passage together. Do you understand?"

"I don't like it. But good sense tells me I have no choice."

"I have acknowledged that the boy is our son. You are his father. I am his mother. You must accept that eventually." She turned to the boy. "Flying Crow, look at this man's hair and his eyes. Someday, you will understand better. But this man is your blood father. You are going to learn to know him in the years ahead. He is a good man, and you will come to love him as he already loves you."

"Josh," she continued, "your son speaks near perfect English, and Tabby is working with me to teach him to read and write. These skills, along with his coloring, assure he will someday have a place in the white man's world. When we come to the reservation, you can no doubt take him by force. I do not even know what my place will be when that happens. If we do not fight each other, though, we can share a son, and his life will be better for it. You have suffered great pain in losing him and your wife. But you, at least, have found your son. I promise you will not lose him again. I would not do that to you . . . or him. In the meantime, I will prepare him for a smoother entry into his life. Can you trust me to do this?"

"I think you'd better think about taking up lawyering when you get to the so-called civilized world. Yeah, I trust you, but I don't really have any choice."

Late that afternoon, Josh, Cal and Sergeant Ezekiel Hooper left the Comanche encampment and started their journey across the Staked Plains. It was with a feeling of sadness that Josh left his sister and son behind. He took some comfort, however, from a crow feather a little rusty-haired Comanche boy had shyly placed in his hand at their departure, and which was now nestled in his front shirt pocket over his heart.

About the Author

Ron Schwab is the author of *Sioux Sunrise, Paint the Hills Red, Medicine Wheel, Night of the Coyote,* and *Last Will,* the latter two of which were nominated for Best Novel Peacemaker Awards by Western Fictioneers. He is a member of the Western Writers of America, Western Fictioneers, and Mystery Writers of America.

Ron and his wife, Bev, divide their time between their home in Fairbury, Nebraska and their cabin in the Kansas Flint Hills.

To learn more about Ron and his books, please visit www.RonSchwabBooks.com.

Made in the USA
Las Vegas, NV
04 October 2023

78571210R00152